SECRET JAGUAR

STACY CLAFLIN

SECRET JAGUAR
CURSE OF THE MOON - BOOK SIX
by Stacy Claflin
http://www.stacyclaflin.com

Copyright ©2017 Stacy Claflin. All rights reserved.
©Cover Design: Rebecca Frank
Edited by Staci Troilo

This is a work of fiction. Any resemblance to actual persons living or dead, businesses, events, or locales is purely coincidental or used fictitiously. The author has taken great liberties with locales including the creation of fictional towns.

Receive free books from the author:
http://stacyclaflin.com/newsletter

CONTENTS

Chapter One

Carter

I SLID ON MY DARK GLASSES AND TAPPED THE STEERING WHEEL. Should've brought a less conspicuous car. My cherry-red Ferrari did little to help me blend in, and I didn't want anyone to notice me waiting for her across the street from the old hotel.

Too late. I was already there. Just a matter of time before she showed.

Who was she? Finally, I would find out. I had been searching for her for years, but she was well-hidden and alone. And she needed protection. I didn't know anything else about her.

Okay, that wasn't *all* I knew. Not after sensing her presence years earlier and spending so much time trying, unsuccessfully, to find her.

The most important thing to note was that she was a solitary jaguar shifter, and females *never* traveled alone. Seriously, never. Our reality is one of old-world rules, strict consequences, and a hierarchy not all that different from the royalty of the Middle

STACY CLAFLIN

Ages. As such, my father was the king of our family. And he ruled as an aristocrat on steroids.

That was why I had broken away. We didn't see eye-to-eye on anything. He was cruel and heartless, and because I refused to be a dictator, he saw me as weak. Leaving was messy, and we did not part amicably.

If my father discovered a lone jaguar female, he would bring her into the family by any means necessary.

Back to my far-from-inconspicuous Ferrari across the street from the old hotel. And by old hotel, I didn't mean run-down and seedy. I meant it had stood the test of time. It was made of brick and appeared to have once been an impressive mansion.

I studied the front, which had clearly been remodeled to look more modern, but evidence of another era remained.

The front door opened. I sat up straight and readjusted my sunglasses. Was it her or just a regular guest?

I leaned forward and waited, holding my breath. If it was her, I didn't know what I would do. Follow her? Introduce myself? Really, I should've thought this through more. But once I figured out her location—finally—I just jumped into my car and headed over.

Out stepped a tall, slender teenager in a flowered knee-length sundress. Long, wavy light-brown hair cascaded almost to her waist.

The distance between us made it impossible for me to sense if she was the jaguar shifter.

She turned and spoke to someone inside, adjusted a tote bag over her shoulder, then went down the steps.

I scrambled out of my car, closed the door as quietly as I could, and set the alarm. Sure, the small college town was safe but I never took any chances with my Ferrari.

She headed toward the campus. If she was a student, I couldn't figure out why she would be staying in the hotel.

Nothing about this girl made any sense. No wonder it had taken me so long to track her down.

2

If this was even her. I'd have to get closer to determine if she was actually a jaguar shifter. Then if she was, I'd have to figure out what to do. Chances were, she'd fled her birth family. And since she had no other jaguars with her, she probably didn't want anything to do with our kind. Best-case scenario, she'd want nothing to do with me. Worst case, she'd freak out and cause a scene. Maybe even shift right there in the middle of town.

Not that I could blame her either way. Jaguar shifters as a whole were horrible jerks at best. Tyrannical, abusive dictators at worst. And by birth, I was the equivalent of a prince. She'd hate and fear me on principle.

She would be able to sniff out my lineage in half a millisecond. My heart raced as I crossed the street to catch up with her.

Please don't shift out in the open.

Our little town on the Olympic Peninsula was home to more supernatural creatures than I'd ever seen in one place. We'd all managed to keep our true identities hidden, but it would only take one person shifting at the wrong time to drive us all from our homes.

I picked up my pace to a solid jog in order to shorten the distance between us. Her aroma drifted to me on the breeze. Confirmation at last. I inhaled deeply. The sweet perfume of a female jaguar shifter. It reminded me of so many loved ones.

My stomach twisted. I'd had to walk away from them all because of my father and his refusal to let go of the old ways.

No time to dwell on that. The girl in front of me didn't slow or stop or even seem to notice me. How could she miss the scent of a jaguar shifter so close?

Had she so immersed herself into the human life that her animal senses had dulled? I'd been away from jaguars for a long time, but I was still deep in the supernatural world. I lived with a pack of werewolves—well, mostly werewolves. We also had some other misfits like myself. In a way, we were all outcasts, some by choice and others not so much.

The female jaguar stopped at a crosswalk. I caught up with her and stood next to her. Her scent enveloped me. She acted like she didn't even notice me.

I turned to her and finally caught her attention. She was breathtaking up close, with deep brown eyes and a sprinkling of freckles across her nose. Being so close to another jaguar, especially one so beautiful, overwhelmed me. It took me a moment to regain my bearings.

I gave a slight noncommittal nod and glanced across the street at the crosswalk signal. Her presence surrounded me, pressing in, threatening to crush me. I hadn't expected this.

The signal finally changed. Her presence didn't.

We walked side-by-side. I struggled to breathe. My bones and muscles ached as my body tried to start a shift. I never shifted against my will.

What was she doing to me?

We reached the campus, and she headed for the courtyard. Beyond that stood more buildings that contained classrooms and labs.

Without notice, she stopped walking. I nearly crashed into her.

She turned to me, wrinkling her nose. Even annoyed, she was gorgeous. "Are you following me?"

"What? No."

Her eyes narrowed and she gave me a once-over. "What are you doing, then? You have no bag, no books. You haven't left my side since the crosswalk."

My usually sharp mind failed me. I couldn't think with this beauty so close to me. Was it because she was the only jaguar shifter I'd seen in years, or because of her personally?

"Well?"

I stood taller. "I'm here to see Professor Foley. I think his office is this way."

Her perfectly manicured brows came together. She didn't believe me. "Professor Foley, huh?"

"Yeah. He's a good friend of mine."

She flipped her hair back and gave me a disapproving look. "Good friend? You're what? A junior or senior? And you're *good friends* with a math professor?"

"It's a little more complicated than that," I admitted. Actually, it was a lot more complicated than that. Tobias Foley was married to the only woman I'd ever loved—loved, as in past tense. And he was also the alpha of my misfit pack of werewolves, vampires, a jaguar shifter, and a missing valkyrie. *Complicated* didn't begin to explain it.

The jaguar shifter in front of me stepped back. "Are you following me?"

How could I answer without lying? "Do you know where Toby's office is?"

Her expression softened. "Toby, huh? Maybe you do know him, but if you're so close, why don't you know where his office is?"

"Do you know where the office of everyone you know is?"

She shrugged and bore her gaze into my eyes. "If I'm as close to them as you claim you are with Mr. Foley, then yes, I would know where their offices are."

"Well, I've never been to his office, but I know where he lives." More than that. I'd kissed his wife. But not when she was his wife —I'm not that kind of guy. She didn't know him at the time. Well, she did, but she didn't. Like I said, complicated. I wouldn't kiss her now.

"Oh, yeah? Where?"

"In a mansion. You know where it is?"

She shook her head. "I've only heard the rumors going around."

Oh, yes. The rumors.

"Are you one of his foster kids?"

I slid my sunglasses to the top of my head. "No."

She glanced up at the enormous clock on a nearby building. "Well, I gotta get to class. Don't want to be late. You can keep following me if you want. I'm actually heading to his class."

The jaguar shifter was in Toby's class? Did he know she was a jaguar? No, he would've told me. He wouldn't keep something like that from me. But how could he have not noticed?

"You're weird." She spun around and headed back in the direction she was heading.

I caught up with her. "No, I'm not."

"Whatever you have to tell yourself." She raked her fingers through her hair, sending fresh waves of her mesmerizing aroma my way. "Oh, and for the record, after you find Professor Foley, no more following me."

"Sure, whatever. And I'm not following you. Or, I wasn't until you invited me to." Guilt stung at me for lying, but it just popped out. And I sure as heck wasn't going to admit it.

We wandered through the campus in silence. Her sweet scent kept wafting my way, making it hard for me to think straight. Thankfully, she didn't want to talk.

I followed her into a building, up some stairs, and finally into a classroom. Without another word, she grabbed a seat and pulled out her phone, making a point that she wasn't paying me any attention.

More than anything, I wanted to run. I knew where she was, and now I had to get away. It was impossible to think clearly around her. If I was going to figure out what to do next, I had to get as far away from her as I could.

Toby walked into the room. He gave me a double-take. "Carter? What are you doing here?"

My 'friend' glanced up from her phone. Her eyes were wide and her expression surprised.

I felt like saying, *See? I know him.* Instead, I turned back to Toby and stepped closer. "I found that jaguar shifter."

"You did? As in, you actually saw her?"

"Yeah. As it turns out, you've been seeing her every day." I nodded toward her. "The floral sundress."

Toby glanced over. "Katya Pelletier? I've never gotten any supernatural vibes from her."

Well, at least he hadn't been keeping her a secret from me. Especially since he knew how hard I'd been looking for her.

"You'll have to tell me more tonight. I've got to start class."

I nodded, then turned to leave but I glanced over at the mysterious jaguar shifter one more time.

Katya.

Chapter Two

Katya

I STARED AT PROFESSOR FOLEY, BUT COULDN'T MAKE SENSE OF anything he said. He may as well have been speaking Greek. I couldn't stop thinking about Carter. That was what Professor Foley had called him when he walked in.

It had surprised me. I mean, I totally thought Carter was lying about knowing my professor. It wouldn't have been the first time some guy had stalked my schedule and pretended to have something in common with me.

There was also something different about Carter. I couldn't put my finger on it exactly, but whatever it was made it so I couldn't think about math—and I needed to pass the upcoming exam.

Sure, Carter was hot, but that hardly made him stand out. There was an unusually high concentration of good-looking guys around here. Definitely not like anywhere else I'd lived.

"Katya?"

I snapped my attention back to Professor Foley. "Yes?"

Giggles sounded around me.

"Do you know the answer?"

My face burned. "Sorry, no."

"Maybe you should pay attention, then." He gave me a friendly smile.

I nodded but didn't respond. Usually, he gave stern expressions to people who zoned off in class. Was it because of Carter that he was being so generous?

Ugh. I needed to get that guy off my mind and just focus on math. Carter who?

I managed to pull myself together and pay attention to the lecture. The next time Professor Foley called on me, I gave him the right answer before he finished asking.

After class, I gathered my things and headed for the door, desperate for some fresh air. Thankfully, I had the next hour free.

Professor Foley stepped in front of me. "Is everything okay, Katya?"

I forced a smile. "Just a little distracted. It won't happen again."

"If you ever need to talk, I'm here."

Now my professor wanted me to talk about my life with him? Had I entered into some kind of alternate universe?

He cleared his throat. "If you have any math questions, stop by my office. I'm happy to help."

I stared at him, trying to make sense of everything. Unfortunately, nothing made sense since Carter happened. How could so much change in such a short time?

"Thanks." I hurried out of the classroom and made my way outside. The warm sun comforted me. I pulled out my earbuds, stuck them into my phone, and listened to some music. Then I strolled over to a large oak tree I'd started to think of as mine. At least in the hour between math and art.

I sat at the base and closed my eyes, losing myself in the music. Once it switched over to a song I didn't like, I opened my eyes. And practically jumped out of my skin.

Across the courtyard, Carter sat at a bench. He was looking at his phone, but what was he *really* doing there? Was he following me again?

I studied him. He was possibly more gorgeous than any other guy on campus. He was tall, tan, and well-built. It was like he spent his entire life at the gym. From where I sat, his short, dark hair exactly matched his intense eyes. Some tattoos stuck out from under his short shirtsleeve.

Carter was probably used to girls falling over themselves to impress him. He had a serious wakeup call coming if he expected *me* to react that way.

What I needed to do was to march over to him and demand to know what was going on. Why was he following me? And did he have something to do with why Professor Foley had given me a kind smile after I'd gotten lost in thought in the middle of class? It was all because of Carter, but none of it made any sense.

I mentally prepared myself to walk over and demand answers. He turned toward me and smiled. I stuffed my earbuds and phone into my bag and took a deep breath. What was his deal? Did he think I had a shortage of stalkers? Counting him, I had one. And that was one too many.

Once I was done questioning him, he could take his sexy, tattooed, muscular self as far away from me as possible. I certainly didn't need the drama.

He continued to hold my gaze as I made my way over to him.

Someone grabbed my arm. I spun around, surprised. Jessie, Lola, and Paige swarmed me.

"Where have you been?" Paige demanded.

"Did you hear the news?" Lola exclaimed.

"I can't believe it!" Jessie clasped her hands.

I stared at them. "What are you guys talking about?"

Paige pulled me over to a picnic table. "You didn't hear? Oh-em-gee, Katya! Best news ever."

"What is?" My mind raced, trying to figure what they could be talking about.

"Seattle—they're out."

I gave her a double-take. "You mean the volleyball team?"

"Yeah!" Lola squealed. "A couple of their players were caught with drugs. They're out of the playoffs."

The gravity of the situation sank in. A thrill ran through me. "That means *we're* in!"

"Exactly!" Jessie held her palm out, and we all exchanged high-fives.

I twisted my hair over my shoulder. It was a nervous habit. "When do we start practicing?"

Paige smiled. "Today. The coach set up daily sessions. Did you drop your phone in the toilet or something?"

"No." I dug around in my bag to find it. "I was in class."

Jessie shook her head. "The whole team has been texting all morning. You seriously missed the all the conversation?"

I finally found my phone underneath my math book—it felt more like a stack of bricks. "I had a big fight with Alley last night, so I silenced it."

"Couldn't you just block her?" Lola asked. "This is huge. Too huge to miss because you were avoiding someone."

"I know it is!" My thoughts raced. "I had no idea we stood a chance of being in the finals."

This was great news, not only for our team but also because it gave me the perfect excuse to avoid my sister and stop thinking about Carter. Between classes and practices, I would barely have time to eat and sleep, much less worry about anyone else.

I glanced over the texting conversation as we sat and discussed the playoffs for a few minutes before going our separate ways.

"Turn on your ringer," Lola called.

I held up my phone and flipped the little bar over. "It's on!"

She gave me a thumbs-up and spun back around. I leaned against the picnic table and read the massive texting thread more closely.

The first one was from our co-captain, telling everyone about Seattle's bad news but our good news. Then everything exploded with questions and verbal high-fives until the coach confirmed what everyone wanted to hear. We were in the playoffs. It was official.

I couldn't stop smiling. We'd worked so hard, only to be defeated right before the playoffs. If Seattle hadn't beaten us, we'd have made it. But thanks to their drug use, we were in!

By the time I was done reading through all the texts, it was almost time to head to art. I sent a quick reply expressing my excitement and explained that my phone had been off. Then I put my phone away and glanced around.

The bench where Carter had been sitting was now empty. A wave of disappointment washed over me. What was wrong with me? He was a stalker. Not someone I had feelings for.

I pushed the disappointment aside and ignored it. The fact that he was nowhere to be seen only made my day better. I didn't need that annoying hottie distracting me from the playoffs.

The playoffs! Still grinning from ear to ear, I headed over to my art class. Though the day had started out horribly—I hated fighting with my sister, and I certainly didn't need a stalker—everything had turned around in a matter of minutes.

Chapter Three

Carter

I FINISHED MY BARBECUE STEAK SUB AND WATCHED THE building Katya had gone into for her next class. She hadn't seen me follow her. I was starting to feel a little creepy but pushed aside the feelings because she needed me. There were no other jaguar shifters in the area, but if any did come, she was unprepared for them. Without my help, they would snatch her up and she'd never be able to get away from them.

There was probably another half hour before her class was over. I tossed my wrapper into the garbage and decided to use the time to explore the building and maybe find her classroom.

I still couldn't believe that after all this time of sensing another jaguar in the area, I'd finally found her. Clearly, she wasn't excited about me, but that was only because I hadn't had a chance to show her I was different from all the others.

A group of girls walked by and waved at me, giggling. I waved back, even though I didn't know any of them, and then I headed into the building.

It was just a normal building. I didn't know what I was expecting. Huge signs pointing the way to her class? Right.

I sniffed the air. Her scent lingered, mixed with everyone else's. It seemed to head toward the stairs, however it was difficult to tell, given that it was faint and mixed with others. I probably shouldn't have waited so long to come inside.

Following nothing other than a hunch, I headed up the stairs.

And there she was.

I skidded to a stop. Katya stood in the hallway talking to a blonde girl. They were both in cheer uniforms. That gave me pause. She'd entered the building in a dress, and now she wore that? It seemed odd that they would have practice in this building and not the gym.

Not that it mattered. Now I had the chance to get off on a better foot with her. See if I could find out her story—what brought her to the area away from her shifter family. Leaders didn't give up any of their family members without bloodshed. That was how I'd gotten my freedom. I shuddered at the thought.

I took a deep breath and considered my wording carefully as I approached Katya and her friend.

The friend noticed me first. She flipped her blonde hair and waved, smiling widely. "Hey, there. Are you new around here?"

I smiled back. "I am, if by 'here' you mean the building."

The blonde stuck her hand out. "I'm Brenna."

"Nice to meet you, Brenna." I continued smiling but kept my attention on Katya.

"Oh, definitely." Brenna gave me a once-over. "I hope to see you around. Are you going to the party on Friday?"

I glanced over at her. She slid her finger around her phone's screen, not seeming to pay us any attention. "I haven't heard about it yet."

Brenna's face lit up even brighter. "Oh? Give me your number, and I'll text you all the details."

"Sure." I recited the numbers, and she put them into her phone. "Got it. I'll send the deets to you soon. Very nice to meet you." She held my gaze a few moments longer than necessary and turned to Katya. "See you at practice later."

She glanced up from her phone. "Yeah, definitely. See ya."

Brenna left, keeping her gaze on me until she disappeared around a corner.

I cleared my throat and tried to think of something to say that would help me get onto Katya's good side. "So, are you going to the party on Friday?"

She finally put her phone away. "You want me to?"

The directness of her question surprised me. "Well, I'll go if you're there."

"Really?" She put her phone away and grinned. "If I go?"

I nodded. Something was different about her, but I couldn't figure out what it was. Maybe it was just the cheer outfit. She hadn't struck me as the cheerleading type before. That had to be it.

"Yeah. Why does that seem strange?"

Katya gave me the once-over and then nodded slowly. "Well, of course I'll be there. The whole squad will be there. And most of the football team."

"Are you going with anyone?"

She shook her head no. "I'll keep an eye out for you, though."

"Great." I relaxed, glad to have finally gotten on her good side. "I'll look for you, too."

She pulled her hair back into a ponytail. "Perfect. What did you say your name is?"

"Carter." I extended my arm.

"I'm—"

Three more cheerleaders ran down the hall, laughing. One of them grabbed her arm and pulled her away.

"I'll see you at the party!" I called.

She waved, already immersed in conversation with her teammates.

I waved back, then headed outside. It was a nice day, and I

didn't feel like heading home, so I sat at the base of a tree and soaked in the sun's rays.

The day had gone better than I'd expected. I certainly hadn't anticipated Katya opening up to me so quickly. The suddenness was a little jarring, but maybe seeing her friend's approval of me had helped warm her up.

My cousin Rachel texted me. The timing of it concerned me. I'd just met a local jaguar, and now someone from my dad's family reached out right away?

It made me think maybe I hadn't cut my ties as permanently as I'd thought. Or maybe it was just a coincidence. Sometimes Rachel called just to see if I was okay. We'd been pretty close growing up.

That had to be it. I was being unnecessarily jumpy. They weren't watching me, and they weren't watching Katya. Of course they didn't care about her. She wasn't even part of the family group.

Except that they'd be more than happy to take in a lone female jaguar. Anger ran through me. They'd force her away from her life, marry her off to a cruel man, and never let her go.

I sat up straight, more determined than ever to keep Katya safe. Even if she didn't want anything to do with me, I'd find a way to protect her from them and every other jaguar shifter out there. Luckily, she was talking to me.

Rachel filled me in on our family and I texted back, my mind on Katya. I was always careful to keep details of my life secret, even from those I trusted. It wouldn't take much for my father to force it out of them if he ever decided he wanted me back in the family.

After Rachel ended the conversation, I read through it several times trying to find anything between the lines warning me about them knowing about Katya.

Nothing stood out.

I breathed a sigh of relief, stuck my phone back into my pocket, closed my eyes, and leaned against the tree.

When I opened my eyes, I felt rested.

Crap! I'd fallen asleep. Grumbling, I rose and checked to make sure my phone and wallet were still safely in my pants. They were.

It was now into the afternoon. I'd slept about two hours, which meant I'd probably lost any chance of running into Katya again. She could be at the gym, at the hotel, in the library, or in class. There was no way to tell now.

I headed for Toby's office, stopping in the bathroom first. On the way to the urinal, my reflection in the mirror caught my attention. Someone had stuck a daisy behind my ear while I slept.

And I'd walked halfway across campus like that, nodding hellos to more than a couple dozen people.

I pulled out the flower, but realized it could've been worse. Someone could've drawn on my face with markers. That would've been more embarrassing than a flower. People had probably just thought a girl had stuck it there.

Maybe one had. Could it have been Katya?

I stuck the daisy back behind my ear, took care of business, and headed for Toby's office. As I stepped off the elevator at his floor, Katya appeared from the staircase.

That wasn't the weird part. Now she was wearing a volleyball uniform.

She scrunched up her face. "Are you following me?"

"No, I just wanted to talk with To—I, uh, mean Professor Foley." It was so weird referring to him as that.

"Well, you'll have to wait your turn. I have an appointment with him to discuss the upcoming exam."

"Go right ahead." I gestured down the hallway toward his office.

She nodded and walked ahead of me.

I wasn't sure what confused me more. The change in her outfit or her attitude. It was as though we hadn't had the pleasant conversation after Brenna left.

"See you Friday," I said as she knocked on Toby's door.

She turned to me, throwing me a quizzical look. "Friday?"

"Yeah, Friday."

Katya opened her mouth to respond, but Toby's door opened and he waved her in.

He arched a brow at me. "What's up, Carter?"

"Nothing important. I'll talk to you at home."

Katya glanced back and forth between us, her brows together. She appeared as baffled by me as I was by her. I probably shouldn't have mentioned anything about living with Toby. If she didn't know he was married, who knew what she would have thought now?

Chapter Four

Katya

I THREW MYSELF ONTO MY BED AND CLOSED MY EYES. EVERY inch of me ached.

It felt wonderful.

We'd practiced harder than ever. The coach had been relentless and it had paid off. We hadn't played that well all year. The team would be ready for the playoffs at this rate. Each one of us knew how lucky we were after having lost the opportunity.

My door opened, but I didn't bother opening my eyes. I didn't want anything to pull me away from the thrill of victory running through my veins.

"We need to talk." Alley's voice broke through my thoughts.

I groaned at my sister and sat up. "I'm not in the mood to fight."

"Me neither. I hate arguing with you. Can we just forget about last night? I was seriously PMS-ing. It was probably all my fault. I even got mad at that cute new bellhop."

My mouth gaped. She was taking the blame?

She shoved me playfully and sat on my bed. "I know, write down the date. I'm wrong for once." She laughed. "So, what are you doing in your gear?"

I glanced down at my volleyball uniform. "Didn't you hear? We're in the playoffs."

My sister tugged on her cheer skirt. "But Seattle beat you guys."

"They had some help." I couldn't keep the laughter out of my voice. "And they also got caught. We're in!"

"Congratulations!" Her expression lit up, matching mine. Seriously, she exactly matched my expression. We were identical twins with the same face but totally different personalities.

"Alley-Kat!" Our mom's voice drifted from down the hall.

"When will she drop that stupid nickname?" Alley rolled her eyes. "We're not five anymore. It's so not cute."

"At least she doesn't do that around our friends."

"I guess." Alley stuck her head out into the hall. "We're in here."

Mom came in, carrying a clipboard. "Can you girls—?" She stared at me. "What's with the uniform?"

"Right?" Alley gave me an I-told-you-so expression. "That's what I said."

I explained the playoffs to Mom. She then enveloped me in a hug. "I'm so happy for you." She turned to Alley. "Are you going to cheer at the games?"

"Probably. I'm not sure the coach knows yet. She didn't say anything today."

"Well, let me know the dates, and I'll make sure someone covers for me." Mom turned back to her clipboard. "Any chance either of you can help out at the front desk now? Sally had to leave early because one of her kids is sick."

I glanced over at my bag full of homework waiting to be done. "I can help if you'll let me do my homework."

"I'll pay you double for the trouble."

Alley jumped in between us. "I'll help too."

Mom beamed. "You girls are the best. How did I ever get so lucky?"

Lucky? She was a single mom who had to work every waking moment to keep our creepy hotel running. With everyone else she had to hire, there was no room left in the budget for someone to help her manage everything.

She headed out the door. "Be sure to change before heading down to the front desk. We have a big group coming soon to check in. Can't have anyone looking unprofessional."

Alley and I exchanged a knowing look. We knew the drill. Having lived in the old mansion-turned-hotel for the last five years, helping take care of it was second nature.

Twenty minutes later, both of us sat behind the long counter wearing matching pantsuits and professional smiles for the guests. Behind the desks, we both had a pile of school books along with our laptops. During the lulls, we could do homework.

Alley yawned. "I'm so tired. The coach really worked us today."

"Yeah, I kind of feel the same way, except I'm way too excited about being in the playoffs to feel it. It's the best day."

"I know." She threw me a friendly smile. "I'm so happy for you."

Ding-dong.

The bell over the front door. We both turned our attention to the group coming in and got everyone registered.

By the time we finally had some breathing room to do homework, I was just as wiped out as my twin. We pulled out our things and got to work.

Alley yawned again. "I'm grabbing some coffee. Want some?"

I shook my head. "I'll never get to sleep if I do."

"Sometimes it's hard to believe we're supposed to be exactly the same." She yawned again. "Even with the caffeine, I'll fall asleep as soon as I hit the pillow."

I sighed. "And even with being exhausted and having no caffeine, I'll toss and turn before falling asleep."

"Well, you want some hot chocolate or something instead? That's relaxing, isn't it?"

"It still has caffeine. Thanks, though."

Alley shrugged and went around the desk to the row of vending machines for coffee. She came back with a steaming cup and a couple bags of Skittles, handing me one of the bags. "That won't keep you up, will it?"

"Nope. Thanks." I opened it as I turned back to my laptop.

"What are sisters for?"

The lull dragged on for a while, giving us a long stretch of time to get some homework done. I made it all the way through my art history assignment before the bell over the door made any more noise.

"Carter?" Alley asked.

My head snapped up. Sure enough, it was my sexy stalker.

He glanced back and forth between us, his face pale and his expression confused.

"You know him?" I asked Alley.

"Yeah." She kept her attention on him and waved him over.

Well, that explained it. I should've known it was a case of mistaken identity. I'm not sure why the thought hadn't crossed my mind earlier.

"There are two of you?" Carter asked.

I put my laptop away. "Yep. You thought I was her this morning."

Alley turned to me, arching a brow.

Carter leaned against the counter. "Which one of you is Katya?"

"Me." Now I was confused. He hadn't thought I was Alley?

He studied me. "You're the one who took me to Toby's classroom?"

"Right."

Alley turned to me. "You're on a first-name basis with a professor?"

I shook my head. "Carter is. You live with Professor Foley?"

He drew in a deep breath and glanced back and forth between us, stopping at Alley. "What's your name?"

"I thought I told you." My sister's tone held annoyance. It wasn't often guys forgot her. "I'm Alley."

Carter shook his head. "You started to tell me, but then your friends grabbed you and dragged you away."

"Oh, right." Pink colored her cheeks.

I was tempted to snap a picture. Alley almost never got flustered, and she'd probably deny it later.

"Are you the one who invited me to the party on Friday?"

Alley grinned, her color returning to normal. "Well, technically it was Brenna, but yeah, we were talking about meeting up there."

Carter glanced back and forth between the two of us. "Are you both...?" His voice trailed off.

"What?" I asked.

He held my gaze and then Alley's but didn't answer my question.

"Both what?" I repeated.

"Never mind. I'm just confused."

Alley and I exchanged a glance before she turned back to Carter. "So, what brings you here? Planning on staying in the hotel?"

"I was looking for you, but I didn't realize there were two of you."

Alley giggled. "That does make things awkward. Did you come to talk about Friday?"

Carter glanced back and forth between us, seeming unsure how to answer. His confusion was actually kind of adorable. He came off as so confident and sure of himself earlier. Now he seemed so... human.

Ding-dong.

Another group of people. I groaned. That might take us half an hour to get everyone settled before we could get back to our homework, and I was already behind.

Carter stepped aside and nodded toward some chairs by the vending machines. "I'll just be over there."

Alley and I turned our attention to the guests. The largest man of the group, who also ordered everyone else around, froze when he saw Carter. The two of them stared each other down as soon as Carter noticed him.

Alley leaned close to me. "Awkward."

"Awkwardness seems to follow Carter around."

"Yeah, but I'll take that kind all day long." She stared at him longingly.

I sighed.

She turned to me. "Wait, you don't like him, do you? I didn't even think about that."

Of course she didn't. Whenever guys had the choice between this set of twins, they always chose Alley. "No, he's annoying."

Alley arched a brow. "Why do I get the feeling you're lying?"

"I'm not."

"If you like him, just say so. I won't go to the party with him. There will be tons of guys there. I don't want to hang out with the one you have feelings for."

My face flamed, though unlike her, it wasn't all that unusual. "I *don't* have feelings for him."

"Really?" Her tone told me she didn't believe me. "Hey, I know. Why don't you come to the party? Or do you have a hot date already?"

I glared at her. "You know I don't."

"Then come. He probably thought you invited him since he met you first and didn't realize we had the twin thing going on."

I shrugged and glanced over at Carter. He and that big guy from the group were in the farthest corner of the room, and they appeared to be having a heated discussion. Carter's fists were clenched and his expression tight. The other guy was red in the face and gesturing wildly.

My breath caught. What if that guy hit Carter?

"What's going on over there?" Alley sounded more curious

than worried. "He knows everyone, doesn't he? How is it we just met him today?"

Carter spoke to the other man now, and it seemed like he might be the one to throw the first punch.

"Maybe we should call Che." I realized my fists were clenched, and I relaxed them. "He might need to break up a fight."

"Go ahead." Alley's attention didn't leave Carter and the other man. "I want to watch this."

"Fine." I dug out my phone and texted Che, who was twice as intimidating as the big guy arguing with Carter.

He showed up a few minutes later and carried the man's bags to his room, pulling him away from Carter.

Alley turned to me. "That was so intense. What do you think it was about?"

I glanced back over at Carter, who now stared out the large picture window.

"I have no idea, but I want to find out."

Chapter Five

Carter

I TOOK DEEP BREATH AFTER DEEP BREATH, BUT IT DID NOTHING to calm me. Fury tore through me like I had never felt.

Not only was a jaguar shifter family in town, but they were staying in the same hotel as Katya and Alley. There was no way the group didn't know the girls were jaguars—or was only Katya the shifter?

This whole time, I had only ever sensed *one* shifter in the area. Katya had smelled of jaguar the whole time I'd spoken with her, but I couldn't recall the sweet scent when talking with Alley. I hadn't been paying close attention because I'd had no reason to think she wasn't Katya.

I pulled out my phone and texted Toby, explaining the situation.

Carter: There's no way I can leave her here alone with those jags.

Toby: Want me to send over Alex and Bobby?

I hesitated before responding. Would throwing two werewolves into the mix help or hurt the situation? It might piss off the other jaguar shifters, but at least they'd be there as backup if anything did go down.

Carter: Yeah. I'll book us a room.

Toby: OK. They'll be there soon.

I put my phone away and turned back to the front desk. Both Katya and Alley were watching me. Probably curious about the verbal altercation with the jaguar alpha I'd just had. I took a deep breath and hurried over.

"Everything okay?" The one on the left asked. I thought it was Katya. That's where she had been standing before. It was hard to tell, though. Those two looked exactly alike.

I sniffed the air. The jaguar aroma came from her, but not Alley.

How could they be identical twins, but only one was a jaguar shifter?

A woman who looked like an older version of the twins merged from a back room behind the counter. "You girls can head up to your rooms now. Thanks for helping."

I sniffed the air again. No jaguar scent from her, either. The twins' dad had to be a jaguar shifter. That was the only explanation. It was rare that shifters and humans mated, but when they did, it was hit or miss if the kids ended up shifters or human.

If Katya and Alley's dad was a shifter, maybe the visiting jaguars weren't a threat, even though the alpha didn't like me. Jaguar families rarely got along with other families.

Maybe I didn't need to spend the night at the hotel, after all. If the visiting shifters were here for the dad, they wouldn't harm Katya. Plus, her dad would watch over her.

The twins gathered their things and came over.

Their mom turned to me. "Will you be staying here, young man?"

She obviously didn't realize I was a jaguar shifter like her husband.

Ding-dong.

A family of five strolled in. They smelled human.

27

"Maybe."

"You don't know?" She raised an eyebrow.

"Not yet." I strolled over to a couch.

Katya and Alley followed me, each one sitting next to me.

"What was that all about?" Alley asked. I could only tell because she didn't smell like a jaguar shifter. "Were you arguing with that big guy?"

"We had some words, that's all."

"About what?"

"Family matters."

"You're related to him?" Katya exclaimed.

I shook my head. "No. *Family* matters." I didn't want to speak of shifters with the human family so close.

Both twins stared at me like I'd grown a second head. How could they not know what I meant? I took a deep breath and considered my wording. "You know, like your father's family."

They both widened their eyes.

"What do you know about our dad?" Alley's tone held accusation.

"His *family*."

"You say that like it should mean something." Katya's brows came together.

I studied her. "It doesn't?"

"How would it?" she snapped. "He died when we were three weeks old."

It felt like I'd been punched in the gut. "He did?"

"Yeah." Alley glared at me. "What do you know about him? We hardly know anything about him. How is it you do?"

My head swam, trying to make sense of the new information. "You don't know *anything* about him?"

Katya bit her lower lip. "We have some pictures."

"And the stories Mom has told us. He wasn't close to his family."

I stared at her. "He wasn't?"

"No. Why do you care? Are you a relative?"

My heart sank. The jaguars who'd just checked in could possibly be their dad's family, and if that was the case, they would want Katya.

They would believe they owned her. Not one of them would flinch at snatching her up and forcing her to marry someone of her dad's status in the family. They'd kill her if she tried to escape.

And they were in this very building.

"Earth to Carter." Alley waved her hand in front of my face.

I just stared at her. My mind was spinning too fast for me to speak. The weight of the situation was too much to take in.

"What's going on?" Katya demanded. "You're starting to scare me."

She *should* have been scared, but I had no idea how much to tell her. I couldn't just tell her she was a jaguar shifter. If she didn't know that world existed, she'd think I was crazy and not want anything to do with me.

Then how would I protect her from a dangerous world she knew nothing about?

Ding-dong.

Alex and Bobby walked through the door. They glanced around and walked over when they saw me.

I finally managed to find my voice, and made introductions. I glared at Alex and Bobby, warning them not to say anything to the twins.

"Are you guys checking in here?" Alley eyed them both, obviously liking what she saw.

Katya continued staring at me with suspicion. She had no idea I was the one person she needed to trust. The jaguar shifters who'd just checked in would have no interest in her sister or mom —just her.

Bobby glanced over at me. "Are we checking in?"

I nodded, everything weighing heavily on me. "We'll take one room. Can you get us registered?" I tossed him my wallet.

He threw it back at me. "I've got one of Toby's cards."

Katya's brows came together. "You guys live with Professor Foley, too?"

Bobby nodded, then headed over to the front desk.

Katya stared at me like I was insane. "I don't know what's going on, but I don't think I like it."

"Wait." Alley turned to me. "You three live in town, but you're staying here?"

Alex sat next to her. "Technically, I'm pretty sure we live just outside of town. But yeah, we want to stay here. It gets crowded over there. There's a bunch of babies and toddlers, and sometimes it's nice just to get away from it all, you know?"

"Babies and toddlers?" Alley rubbed her temples.

I leaned back and closed my eyes. The way things were going, the twins would kick us out before we had a chance to stick around and figure out what was going on with the jaguars.

Alex explained our living situation as best he could without mentioning anything about the supernatural world. If I hadn't been so stressed, I'd have probably found the whole conversation humorous.

"We're all set."

I opened my eyes upon hearing Bobby's voice.

Alley leaned toward him. "Well, if you want to go swimming, be sure to do that before midnight."

"Really?" Bobby sat across from her and raked his fingers through his blond hair. "Why's that?"

"Don't try and scare them," Katya said.

"Now I have to know." Bobby leaned forward. "Why can't we swim after midnight?"

Alley stared at him without saying anything for a moment. "There are accounts of a ghost. She never shows before midnight or after six in the morning."

"I'm listening." Bobby rested his chin on his palm. "Is she dangerous?"

"To men. A bunch of guys have claimed she tried to pull them under. We've had so many complaints that we lock the doors from eleven to seven."

"Then why warn us?"

Katya and Alley exchanged a knowing glance.

Alley turned back to Bobby. "The door has a habit of unlocking itself. We've even tried locking it with a chain on the outside."

"Yeah?"

"The chain disappeared."

Bobby's mouth dropped.

I held back an eye roll. A hotel employee could easily have done that. How hard would it be to unlock a door or hide a chain? Not very, was my guess.

"I'm not going near that pool any time of the day or night." Bobby's face paled.

It was hard not to laugh. I'd seen Bobby face all kinds of enemies with fierce determination, yet he was afraid of the ghost of some girl?

"How old is this building?" Alex asked.

"Nobody really knows." Alley glanced around, keeping her voice hushed. "There are no records of it being built. It was before anyone other than the original owner lived out here. I've even heard rumors of a secret wing."

I couldn't keep my doubt quiet any longer. "A secret wing? How is that even possible? A hidden door or hallway, I could see. But what about outside? Just walk around the perimeter and see the whole building."

Alley shook her head. "It's impossible to get around to the very back. There are thick blackberry bushes, and they run up to the roof."

"Is it just covering a hidden wing, or are the bushes so thick they fill in the gap between two wings?"

Bobby stared at Alley, his mouth gaping wide. "Why would someone hide an entire wing?"

"It's said one of the owners centuries ago sealed it shut after catching her husband having an affair. Neither her husband or the woman were ever seen again. Did she murder them and hide their bodies or kill them by locking them inside the wing?"

Bobby swore. "How do you guys work here without freaking out? I don't even want to stay here anymore."

"Good going." Katya glared at her sister.

The corners of Alley's mouth twitched. "We don't just work here. We live here."

"And you're still alive?"

"No, we're ghosts."

Bobby jumped from his seat.

"She's kidding." Katya burst out laughing.

"You don't live here?" Bobby exclaimed.

Katya threw me an exasperated expression.

I turned to Bobby. "She's kidding about them being ghosts. They aren't dead. Maybe we should get settled into our room."

Alley winked at him. "Unless you want to go swimming with us."

Bobby stumbled backward into the chair and nearly fell over.

Alex laughed. "I've never seen you so freaked out."

"This place is haunted!"

I rose and slapped Bobby on the back. "Come on. Let's find our room."

"It's not near the hidden wing, is it?"

Alley's mouth twisted into a grin. "Nobody knows where that wing is—it's *hidden*."

Bobby's eyes widened. "For real?"

Alley turned to me. "Bring him to the party on Friday night. He's fun."

"I think we have to get through tonight first." I pulled on Bobby and glanced over at Katya, who wouldn't make eye contact with me.

It was going to be tough to protect a girl who was so obviously put off by me. But first, I needed to sniff out the jaguar family and see if I could find out why they were staying in town.

Chapter Six

Katya

I DROPPED MY TEXTBOOK ON THE FLOOR. TRYING TO STUDY WAS a waste of time. I'd read the same paragraph at least eight times and still had no idea what it said. The only thing I could think about was Carter, and that seriously flustered me. Why had he needed to appear in my life? As if I didn't have enough to think about—a mysterious hottie stalker had to show up out of nowhere, claiming to know about my dad.

How could he know anything? Even my mom barely knew anything. She said Dad never liked talking about his family and only ever said he wanted nothing to do with them. It sounded like he thought they were dangerous, but Mom didn't know for sure.

I hated thinking about Dad. It was too frustrating. He held more mysteries than our hotel. Not that I should've been surprised by that. He'd been the one to give Mom the hotel after Alley and I were born.

To add to the intrigue, he never even told her how he'd gotten it. But she'd been so heartbroken after he died that she moved us across the state. We'd only come here five years ago because Mom lost her job and couldn't find a new one. She'd said her only option was to fix up and open Dad's hotel.

Knock, knock.

"Come in," I grumbled. I didn't want to talk with anyone.

Mom came in and sat next to me on the bed. "Are you okay, sweetie?"

I didn't know where to start. Not that I wanted to talk.

"Is it about those three boys you and Alley were sitting with? Were they giving you grief?"

"No." It was the truth. They hadn't done anything wrong. Other than Carter insinuating that he knew about my family. "They just got me thinking about Dad."

She rubbed my back. "I wish you girls could've met him. You'd have adored him, and he would've felt the same way. Did I ever tell you that he named you?"

I gave her a double-take. "No. Why didn't you tell me before?"

Mom frowned. "It hurts so much to think about him."

"Did you name Alley?"

She nodded. "After he picked your name, insisting that your nickname would be Kat, I picked Alley, thinking we could call you two Alley-Kat."

I groaned. "That was on purpose?"

She smiled sadly. "Yeah. I know it annoys you—you're too old for it—but I can't let it go. I feel like it keeps us all connected to Dad." She sighed. "It was cute when you were little, you have to admit."

"I guess. Why did he want me to have the nickname Kat?"

She looked behind me, her gaze turning dreamy for a moment before returning her attention to me. "I'm not really sure. Your dad was a man of many mysteries. I suppose that was a big part of what drew me to him. He seemed to be shrouded in secrets, and I felt special whenever he'd reveal one to me."

"Like what?"

"Family things, mostly."

I froze. After the conversation with Carter and his friends, her wording just didn't sit right with me.

Mom continued, "But even with as long as we were together, and having had you girls, there was still so much I didn't know. I felt like he was holding back on something big. Not to be mean, but more like... Well, I suppose if I knew, it wouldn't be a mystery, would it?"

I scratched my head. "Then why stay with him if he had so many secrets? I can't imagine wanting to be with someone who liked to keep things from me."

She put her hand on mine. "It wasn't like that, Katya. He wasn't *trying* to be deceptive. It was more like..." Her voice trailed away for a moment. "...like there were things he wasn't ready to reveal. I like to think that he planned to tell me everything someday."

"Huh." I tried to imagine the appeal. Carter was mysterious, but it only annoyed me. I couldn't picture myself wanting to stick around and figure it out.

Mom patted my knee and smiled. "It felt like slowly unwrapping a present."

"Ew, Mom. That's my dad you're talking about."

She laughed. "That's not what I meant, but that was fun, too."

I turned away, my face heating. "I don't want to know."

"Okay, sorry. I wasn't trying to go there. I just meant that with him, it felt like every new mystery revealed was bringing me closer to the core secret."

"But you never got that far." I frowned.

Mom shook her head. "Not before he was killed."

"Did you ever have any ideas about how he died?"

"Some, but who's to say how far off they were?"

I scooted closer. "Like what?"

"He got this hotel from his family, so I assume they had money. Or maybe they got a good deal on this place. It was hardly in pristine shape. The thought of the mob crossed my mind once or twice, but he didn't act like your typical mob guy."

"You mean stereotypical?"

"Probably. He wasn't anything like they are in the movies. Honestly, I think it was something else, but we'll never know."

Curiosity burned in my chest. That wasn't just some interesting story, it was *my* history. My family. "Did you ever try to dig deeper? I mean, once he was gone, it wasn't like he could get mad at you."

She met my gaze. "I know, and I have looked several times—for you girls—but I've found nothing. Even with everything available online these days, I haven't come up with anything."

I tapped my finger on the bed, nervous energy buzzing through me. Answers had to be somewhere. Maybe she hadn't looked in the right places. "Have you tried a private investigator?"

"No, honey. Whatever money your dad's relatives have, we don't have access to it. Money's always tight."

"Yeah." I frowned. "But there has to be something we can do. Somewhere else we can find answers?"

She squeezed my hand. "If you start looking, be sensible."

"Sensible? You're talking about my family and my history. I don't just want answers out of curiosity. I need to know."

Her expression tensed. "He was afraid of them. There was a reason I never met them. Look for answers, but promise me you won't look for the people."

How could I make such a promise? I had grandparents, aunts, uncles, and cousins out there who I'd never met. People who could tell me things about my dad that Mom couldn't tell me.

"Katya?"

"Why are they so dangerous?" I countered.

"I don't know, honey."

"And if he didn't want us to find them, why give you this hotel? Isn't that just asking for them to show up one day?"

Mom squirmed. "I don't have the answers. Your dad would've been the one to talk to, and believe me, every day since his passing I've wished he was here for you girls."

I raked my hands through the length of my hair. "Yeah, me too." I stared into her eyes. "What killed him? Why haven't you ever told us? You always dance around the subject or change it altogether."

Tears shone in her eyes and she rose to her feet. "I don't want to talk about this. It's too much."

"Mom! We're almost twenty. Whatever it is, we can handle it. And what's to stop us from looking online?"

"Have you?"

"Yes. There's nothing I can find."

She stared into my eyes, tears running down her face. "He was murdered. Brutally. And I was the one who found him." She ran from the room.

I stared at the closed door with a mixture of emotions raging through me. I'd always assumed Dad had died from an accident or an illness. But a brutal murder? Someone had killed him on purpose? And made him suffer?

Part of me wanted to chase after Mom for more answers, but I couldn't move. Not after hearing that news.

After what felt like forever, I finally gained control of my body again. I reached over to my nightstand and picked up the framed photo of my parents and stared at my dad's smiling face.

He was so happy in that picture. Like his world was complete just having Mom in his arms. She looked so different back then. What would Dad have looked like if he was still alive? More importantly, what would he tell us about our family? Would he have trusted us with the truth?

My bedroom door opened, and I glanced up. It was Alley wearing a silky pajama set.

"You look like you've seen a ghost." She sat on my bed, almost exactly where Mom had been. "Don't tell me that pool ghost came up here."

I turned the picture toward her. "Do you know how Dad died?"

Her face contorted. "Yeah, that he was killed."

"Murdered."

Alley nodded. "I know."

"You *know?*"

She looked away. "Mom wanted to be the one to tell you."

I squeezed my comforter. "Why did she tell you before me?"

"She said she wanted to tell us individually when we were ready."

"I've been ready for a long time!"

"Did you ask?"

I folded my arms. "I was waiting for her to tell me."

"Well, you know now. Isn't that what matters?"

"How long have you known?"

"Katya, don't do this."

"Why not?" I demanded. "How long have you known?"

She sighed. "A while, okay? Just let the news settle. It sucks, and it takes time to process."

I glared at her. How was it that she always experienced everything before me? Everything. And I was the one born first. Where was the justice?

My sister gave me a sympathetic glance, but I wasn't going to accept it. Why did she always get the better end of the deal? First lost tooth, first award, first boyfriend, first everything.

"Katya—"

"Just go."

"We need to talk about this."

I shook my head. "I need space. Please."

"Don't do this."

"Like you said, I need time to process the news." I clenched my jaw. "Let me have that much. You had all the space in the world since I didn't know anything."

"I *wanted* to tell you. More than anything. Twins aren't supposed to have secrets, right?"

"Apparently we do." I shot her an icy stare.

"That's not fair. Mom made me keep it a secret."

"Seems our family's full of those. You could've told me if you'd wanted." I turned my back to her and waited for the sound of the door closing behind her.

Angry tears blurred my vision. I blinked them away, then

turned around and looked at my room. The walls seemed to close in on me. This little corner of the massive building had been my refuge for the last five years, but now it was more like a prison.

Fuming, I grabbed a light hoodie from my closet and headed out into the hallway. It wasn't like I was going to get any homework done in my current state of mind.

Silence greeted me. I walked down the hall and leaned against the wall to try and catch my breath. My fury made it hard to breathe normally. I glanced down both directions. I could go to the left and pass the guest rooms and other more public areas.

Or I could go to the right and eventually wind up in the areas where guests weren't allowed. Places that hadn't been renovated and brought to code.

Places that might be sealed off, holding secrets that could reveal answers to my own past. A fake wall or hidden door that could lead me to a wing unseen for centuries.

I took a deep breath and turned right.

Chapter Seven

Carter

"What's the plan?" Bobby looked at me like I had a masterful plan.

"Keep Katya safe while figuring out why those jaguar shifters are here. This whole area has been jaguar-free for years."

"Other than you." Bobby smirked.

"Easy to be brave when there isn't the ghost of a teenage girl, right?" I snapped.

He glared at me. "What's gotten into you?"

"Jaguar shifters! I don't think Katya even knows that she's anything other than human. It sounds to me like her dad never told anyone about his real heritage."

"Do you think those jaguars have been looking for her?" Alex asked.

I clenched my fists. "I don't see any other reason they'd be here."

"It could be a coincidence." Alex tilted his head. "This whole area is full of supernaturals."

"But not jaguars."

"So, what's the *plan*?" Bobby repeated.

"I'm going to find out what I can about them and also about Katya."

"Can't you just tell her she's a shifter?" Alex was a wolfborn, and had spent the majority of his life in the wolf form, only becoming human when other werewolves shifted into their animal form. He was still learning about the human world and had a long way to go. I was just grateful jaguars didn't rely on lunar cycles for shifting anymore.

"Not without her thinking I've lost my mind. And I don't want to freak her out by shifting in front of her." I rose and cracked my knuckles. "Why don't you two follow me? But stay a distance behind. I don't want the jags to get a whiff of you." To say that traditional jaguar shifters hated werewolves was the understatement of the century. It had been like that for centuries.

They both nodded.

"Do you know where they're staying?" Bobby asked.

"I will once I sniff them out." I pressed my ear against the door. "It's clear. Wait no more than a minute before coming out. Track my scent."

They both nodded, then I slipped out into the hallway. It was a nicely kept hotel, and I liked the old charm, though it did kind of creep me out. What if there really was an entire wing nobody could find? What secrets would be found there?

I shook my head to clear it. I needed to focus. This wasn't a ghost hunt. There was a lone female jaguar shifter who didn't realize how much danger she was in. And I was the only one who could help her.

Closing my eyes, I listened. Muffled conversation sounded down the hallway in both directions. I sniffed the air. The jaguar scent was impossible to miss with so many having checked in. It irritated my nose since they weren't from my family.

I followed that odor to the left, and it grew stronger. The conversation grew louder. I pressed my ear against each door I passed. None of them appeared to be jaguars. Most of them were talking about a visitor's day on campus.

The perfect cover for the jaguars.

A door opened down the hall, and two male voices sounded. I pressed myself against the wall, not that it would hide me if they came my way. The jaguar scent grew stronger with them in the hallway.

The two guys hurried down the other direction in swim shorts, laughing and shoving each other. They would definitely pass as college hopefuls. No wonder the shifters had brought them.

I waited for them to get far enough ahead that they wouldn't sense me behind them before I crept down the hallway. As I went, I continued listening in each room to see if there were other shifters.

Most were there for the college, and few others were there for different reasons. None of them were jaguar shifters or any other kind of supernatural creature.

I glanced back to see if Alex and Bobby were behind me. They weren't in sight, but I picked up a trace of their scents. At least they were hiding well.

As I pressed my ear against the next door, I froze.

"...told you this place was the one. We all knew Kevin was hiding something from us. Not just a hotel, but a family with humans."

"No wonder he fled, but he paid the price. Nobody leaves and lives. We always find them."

Laughter roared.

A chill ran down my back. Were they planning on killing Katya?

"Well, at least we found out about Kevin's daughter before marrying off Cole. Now he'll get a princess."

"He's got his work cut out for him. That girl doesn't seem to have a clue she's a shifter. Women these days are so rebellious. She's going to have to be broken before she learns her place."

Anger burned in my gut. Sure, I'd suspected their motives, but hearing the confirmation shook me in a way I hadn't anticipated. They had no right stealing her from her life and forcing her to live as a traditional jaguar shifter.

I continued listening, hoping they'd spill their strategy, but the conversation moved on to something else, and then they turned on the TV and stopped talking.

My mind raced. With an entire family of jaguar shifters ready to abduct her, I might have to bring in my entire pack and maybe some other supernaturals. We needed to work together to protect Katya. I couldn't do this on my own.

I bolted down the hall to Bobby and Alex. After filling them in on what I'd heard, I told them to call Toby. "See what he thinks. Should we call in the witches, or maybe see what Tap knows? Actually, one of you should call Tap while the other calls Toby. We don't have time to waste."

They agreed and raced back to our room. I hurried down the hall, eager to find the guys in swimsuits. One of them was likely the guy who thought he was going to marry Katya—then break her.

Not if I had a say in the matter. And with Toby and Tap's resources, the arrogant shifters didn't stand a chance.

I sniffed the air and followed the trail to the jaguar shifters. Interestingly, it led away from the pool.

My skin crawled once I figured that out. What exactly did they have in mind? Were they going to try and take Katya already? Or did they have other plans? Why the swim shorts?

I hated having a ton of questions and no answers.

Their odor led me to the end of the hall, which was roped off. A giant sign warned, 'No Entry. Employees Only.'

Yet the jaguar scent was strong down that way.

I glanced around for any people or cameras, but saw neither. Not that it mattered. If Katya was in danger, I'd risk the wrath of the hotel management.

Ducking under the rope, I sniffed the air again. The scent went to the left. Chills ran down my back as I tiptoed down the dusty hallway. Old framed paintings hung crooked, many covered in cobwebs. Paint peeled and the walls were cracked in several places. The carpet was worn down in places and had plenty of brown stains.

The only thing that made the hallway feel like part of the rest of the hotel was that it had doors spaced apart like the rest. Otherwise, it felt as though I was in a completely different building.

I refocused as the jaguar scent grew stronger. And mixed with a feminine aroma.

Did they already have her?

Without thinking, I burst into a run. The creepy hallway passed in a blur as I allowed myself to go faster than a human could.

I skidded to a stop just as the three of them came into view. They hadn't seen me, and I darted behind a dusty fake potted tree.

Katya was arguing with them, but they stood at an arm's length. They weren't forcing her to go with them. Yet.

I calmed my breathing and listened, trying to make out what they said. It was hard to tell from the distance.

"You... need the... don't understand..."

She responded with a harsh tone, though I couldn't understand a single word.

One of them grabbed her arm. She yanked it back, but he held on.

Such fury ripped through me that I almost shifted right there. It took me a minute to stop that process from starting. By that time, the guy had pinned Katya to the wall, close enough to kiss her.

I fought the shift as I ran right toward the three of them.

"Let go of her!"

They all turned, shock covering their faces. The guy restraining Katya didn't let go.

I punched him across his smug face. "The lady doesn't want you doing that."

"Who are you?" demanded the other guy.

"Your worst nightmare if you don't get out of here right now." I glowered at him, ready to fight the both of them if need be.

"Oh yeah?"

He hit me across the jaw.

Katya cried out.

Everything turned into a blur of fists, elbows, and blows. I tried to restrain myself in order not to freak out Katya, who knew nothing of the supernatural world. But the other two weren't holding back.

I let loose and pummeled them both with all my fury. One of them flew back into the wall, blood gushing from his nose. The other jumped on me, knocking us both to the ground. Before I knew it, they were both pounding on me.

Katya yelled out and pulled on one of the guys, trying to get him off me. He swung at her, but that only made her fight all the harder. He turned his attention from me to her and shoved her against the wall.

More anger surged through me. I pushed the one fighting me then kicked him in the crotch, then the knees. He doubled over and stumbled. I grabbed him by the throat and squeezed as hard as I could. He fought against me, but couldn't remove my hands from him.

I shoved him against his friend, pushing him away from Katya. "You two need to leave her alone. Don't ever let me see you near her again."

The one gasped for air and glared at me. His friend lunged at me. I hit him across the jaw. Blood spurted from his nose, spraying onto my face.

"Leave her alone," I repeated.

He wiped his nose. "You can't watch her every second."

"That's where you're wrong."

We stared each other down until they finally left.

Chapter Eight

Katya

I STARED IN DISBELIEF AT THE TWO JERKS AS THEY WALKED AWAY. Absentmindedly, I rubbed my arm. A bruise was beginning to form from where one of them had grabbed me. It was one of several such places. There was also a rip in the side of my shirt, reaching up to my bra. Luckily, I had a camisole underneath.

What was even more strange was what had gone on inside of me as soon as those two had attacked me. My bones ached. Burned. Something in the pit of my being felt like it wanted to claw its way out. Something raw and animalistic had started to overcome me.

"Are you okay?" Carter's voice broke through my thoughts.

I turned to him. "What just happened?" Not that I expected him to be able to tell me what was wrong with me. The strange experience had happened one other time before—when a guy had tried to take my purse at a bus stop a couple years before. It was like a switch had been flipped. I had walked away with my purse, and he'd limped away, bloody and bruised.

Carter brushed some hair away from my face. Some of it stuck, probably with blood. I was pretty sure it wasn't mine.

"How did you know they were attacking me? This area's off limits to guests."

"Would you believe I sensed trouble?"

I arched a brow. "You *sensed* trouble? What, you sniffed it out like a dog or something?"

"Not quite, but I did see those guys heading this way and I got a bad feeling from them. Turns out I was right."

"Well, either way, thanks."

He smiled, his expression brightening. "Maybe I should thank you. You fought pretty good. I have to say I'm impressed."

My cheeks warmed. This was happening all too often. "Just instinct, I suppose."

"Do you find you have a lot of instincts?"

"What do you mean?" That was an odd question to ask, wasn't it? Sure, I was shaken, but that just didn't seem like a normal question. Or maybe he was just a strange guy. That certainly made sense.

He shrugged. "Nothing. Do you want to get out of here? This place is starting to give me the creeps."

"What? Are you afraid of ghosts?" I grinned.

"Hardly." He stood taller. "This wing just feels like a horror movie in the making. It doesn't help that both of us have blood on us."

I rubbed my cheek where my hair had been stuck. A long streak of dried blood crusted from my mouth to my ear. "True."

"So, what are you doing all the way over here? Looking for that hidden wing?"

I hated that he knew exactly what I was doing. "I should be asking what *you're* doing here. Didn't you see the sign?"

He tilted his head, giving me a sexy look that threatened to melt me into a puddle. "I was following trouble, remember? Do you know what they wanted?"

My entire body stiffened at the reminder of those two. "I think that was pretty obvious. They wanted to—" My voice trembled, and I shook. I couldn't even bring myself to say what they had planned. The look of lust in the one guy's eyes was enough to send a cold chill through me. It was like he thought he had the right to do whatever he wanted to me.

Carter put his arms around me and pulled me close. His embrace was warm and comforting. Even though I didn't know him, I leaned into him and accepted the gesture. His strong arms offered protection, and after what had almost just happened, I couldn't turn it away.

There was something almost familiar about being in his embrace. Not like we'd ever met before that morning, more like he reminded me of someone. I wasn't really sure who, since I'd never had a serious boyfriend. That was more of Alley's expertise. She'd always said I intimidated guys.

Why not Carter? What made him want to follow those guys who he thought were up to no good? Why pull me into a protective hug when I'd done nothing but push him away all day? What was it about him that wasn't intimidated by me?

"Do you want to get cleaned up then grab some coffee?"

I didn't budge. I wanted to stay in his arms indefinitely. "That sounds nice, but caffeine would keep me up all night."

"Tea? A midnight snack?"

I laughed. "Sure. That sounds nice. Is it already midnight?"

"Probably not, but it's hard to tell without any windows in sight. Are you feeling better?"

"Yeah." I stepped back, hating to leave his embrace. If that was what it was like having a boyfriend, I could see why Alley found relationships so appealing.

"Or if you're not in the mood for a snack, we could always look for that secret wing. I'd be lying if I said I wasn't curious."

"That sounds like fun, but another time."

"Is that a date?"

A warm thrill ran through me, but I just gave him a noncommittal "Sure."

Carter put his arm around my shoulders, and we walked back to the main part of the hotel in a comfortable silence. He lifted the rope, letting me go under first, then he followed.

"Where should we get cleaned up?"

I hesitated, nearly saying my room since I needed a new shirt. But after everything I'd just been through I wasn't sure I wanted to tell a guy I'd just met that day where that was—even if he was the one who prevented the assault.

He gave me a reassuring smile. "How about we clean up in our rooms, then meet down in the lobby?"

Suddenly, the idea of going to my room alone seemed like the worst idea ever. The thought of running into those two guys shot fear through me. "Mind if we go to my room? We have bigger bathrooms than the guest rooms."

That sounded so stupid.

He didn't seem to notice. "Sure thing. Lead the way."

We walked past the guest rooms, the lounge, the game room, the small theater, and finally to the end where my family and the staff lived. After we passed the staff rooms, I stopped. Just as I was about to grab my key, Alley stepped out of her room.

Her eyes widened, but then she smiled as her gaze landed on Carter's arm around my shoulder. She'd been bugging me to get a boyfriend for years. Not that Carter was a boyfriend. Or even a potential boyfriend. I didn't know what he was.

"What are you guys doing?" Alley pulled her hair back into a ponytail, then her brows came together. "And why are you guys bloody?"

"You just noticed?"

She gave me a knowing look, obviously trying to tell me that she had been more taken aback because of the guy hanging on my shoulders. "What happened?"

Carter cleared his throat. "There are a couple guests who tried to assault your sister. I stopped them, but you should let the hotel security know."

Alley's eyes widened even more. "What? Are you okay?"

STACY CLAFLIN

I nodded, but didn't reply.

Intensity burned in my sister's expression. "Who was it? We need to tell Che right away."

Carter's arm tightened around my shoulders. "They were with the last family who checked in. Two guys about our age. Do you mind telling Che while I help Katya?"

"Yeah, definitely. I'll make sure he kicks that whole family out on the street!" She pulled out her phone and slid her finger around the screen.

I dug my keys out of my pocket and unlocked my door.

Alley turned to me. "Oh, Selina and Brittney are coming over to swim. Want to join us?" She looked at Carter. "You and your friends are more than welcome."

My stomach tightened at the thought of wearing a swimsuit in front of Carter. I'd never once given it a thought before, never caring who saw me swim. What was this guy doing to me?

"What about the guy-hating ghost?"

Alley laughed. "She won't be out for at least a couple hours—if she even exists."

"I'll let Bobby and Alex know, but I can't guarantee Bobby will want to go anywhere near the pool. I've never seen him squirm like that before." Carter turned to me. "Do you want to go for a swim? Or we can grab a snack like we were talking about. I didn't bring shorts, so I'd just have to sit and dip my feet."

Relief washed through me at not having to wear a swimsuit in front of him. "Either way is fine."

Alley glanced up from her screen again. "Our gift shop has swimwear."

My stomach twisted in knots. Thanks, Alley. I pushed open my door and waved Carter in.

"Have fun, you two." Alley winked at me.

My face flamed. Did she really think we were going to climb into bed? Carter and I had just met!

Once we were both inside, I slammed the door shut and looked around to make sure I hadn't left any underwear laying around. Everything looked clear.

"Bathroom's over there." I gestured toward it.

"Ladies first." Carter sat at my desk and studied my bulletin board full of pictures from my infancy to this year's volleyball team. He zoned in on the one of my dad holding me as a tiny baby.

I wasn't sure if I liked how quickly he made himself comfortable. It sort of bugged me, but at the same time, it didn't. He could fluster me like no other.

"No, I insist. I need to pick out some different clothes first."

He turned to me. "Do you want to go to the pool or not? I should probably let Alex and Bobby know, either way. They might want to go even if I'm not there."

"Even with the potential of a man-hating ghost?"

"If pretty girls are there, he'll risk it."

A spark of jealousy ran through me. It didn't make sense. Why would I be envious of him finding my twin sister pretty? We had the same face. I should've been flattered.

"Do you want to go?" Carter asked again.

I studied him, finding that I was more interested in seeing him in a suit than I was worried about how I looked. "Sure."

Chapter Nine

Carter

BOBBY RAN HOME REAL QUICK AND CAME BACK WITH THREE pairs of swim trunks. He was also more than happy to risk a vengeful ghost if it meant swimming with cheerleaders.

I glanced into the mirror in Katya's bathroom and held out the pair he'd run over to me. They looked clean. I sniffed them. They smelled like a mixture of chlorine and the fabric softener we used at home.

I slid them on, hoping for the best, and then looked at myself in the mirror. No blood anywhere. I waited a minute, not sure how much time I should give Katya to get ready.

"Is it safe to come out?" I called.

"Hold on!"

"Take all the time you need." I spun around and sat on the toilet lid. The bathroom was decorated with a feminine, dark-purple-flowered theme. It even smelled nice. Floral and citrusy.

The bathroom I shared at the mansion with several other guys was nothing like this. It had plain green everything, mismatched towels, and a funky odor that never went away.

"You can come out now," Katya's voice came through the door.

I sprang up and threw open the door. My breath caught in my throat.

She stood in the doorway of her walk-in closet, wearing a thin floral kimono that still showed off the sexy deep-purple one-piece she wore underneath. Her long hair cascaded down over her shoulders like a majestic waterfall.

I struggled to find my voice. "You look beautiful."

Katya's face flushed pink. "So do you." Her face turned red. "Handsome, I mean. Handsome, not beautiful."

She could call me beautiful if she wanted. Actually, she could call me anything she wanted, and I wouldn't care. I wanted so badly to walk over to her, cup her chin, and taste her lips. It took all of my self-restraint not to.

I cleared my throat. "Do you have any towels?"

Holding my gaze, she nodded. "Yeah, but there are also ones down there."

We stood there, staring at each other until she pulled her gaze away. She picked up a hair tie and pulled it onto her wrist. "We should get to the pool. Everyone else is probably there already."

In my mind, I pulled her close, dipped her, and gave her a mind-melting kiss. In reality, I opened the door and waited for her to step into the hallway.

She walked through and waited, holding my gaze. I closed the door behind me, and the lock clicked into place. It took all of my effort to keep from pulling her into my arms.

I'd never felt this way about anyone before, not even when I'd been in love before. And I'd just met Katya, although I'd sensed her presence years earlier and had been searching fruitlessly until today. But meeting her in person was far different from knowing of her existence.

She'd been here in this hotel the whole time. How had I not known?

Katya cleared her throat. "So, uh, are you ready?"

"Yeah, let's go." Hopefully I sounded as relaxed as I tried. It was growing increasingly hard to think clearly around her.

We headed downstairs to the main lobby. I wanted to put my arm around her again, but feared that if I did, I couldn't keep myself from kissing her.

A commotion sounded near the front desk. The entire jaguar shifter family stood with their bags, arguing with a tall, muscular guy wearing a shirt with the hotel logo on the front.

One of the guys I'd fought pointed to me. The father—the alpha—shot me a death glare. I returned it with a threatening stare of my own. If he thought he could intimidate me that easily, he was sadly mistaken.

By nature, I was an alpha myself. Had I not walked away from my own family, I'd have been in training to lead our group once my father passed away. Not only that, but my new family was a strong pack who had defeated many enemies far scarier than this dude.

No way would I back down. They were not going to drag Katya into their lifestyle. I'd fight them to the death if it came down to it. And I wouldn't hesitate to bring in other powerful supernaturals, either.

They had no clue who they were dealing with. Whether Katya and I fell in love or not, I would make sure she remained as far away from these monsters as possible. Especially since she had no idea about her true nature.

How she'd managed to go this long without shifting was beyond me. It was impossible to avoid once puberty struck. Unless not knowing made it possible.

Katya stepped closer to me as the hotel employee escorted the pack of jaguar shifters outside. One of her attackers turned toward her and made an inappropriate gesture.

I put my arm around her and fought back a shift. With all these almost-shifts, my body would go crazy if I didn't turn into my jaguar form soon. Once I was certain Katya was safely asleep, I'd head out into the woods for a run.

Maybe I'd even find one of those losers and tear him apart. My pulse pounded at the thought.

Katya shook. I smoothed her hair down with my palm and whispered in her ear, "They're gone now. They can't hurt you."

"I sure hope you're right."

"They won't."

She looked up at me. "How can you be so sure?"

"I'll make sure of it. If I need to sleep outside your door, I will."

The hotel employee came back inside without the jaguar shifters. He glanced at Katya. "I told them if they show up here again, we'll call the cops, no questions asked."

"Thank you, Che."

He stepped closer, holding her gaze. "What happened, exactly?"

Katya shook some more. I tightened my arm around her shoulders.

"I need to know," Che said.

I glared at him. "She doesn't want to talk about it."

He glared back. "Then why don't you tell me?"

"Okay. They followed her to a wing that was marked as off-limits to guests. I could tell they were up to no good, so I followed them. Turns out I was right."

Che turned back to Katya. "You know your mom doesn't want you back there."

She stepped forward and stared him down. "I'm an adult. And don't forget, my dad left this hotel to my sister and me. I can go wherever I want!"

He jutted his jaw but didn't respond.

I stepped up to Katya and put my arm around her again. "Would you make sure she remains safe?"

"Of course, that's my job."

The way he said *job* struck me as odd. I sniffed the air. A distinct male jaguar scent hung in the air. It was too strong to be merely lingering from the group that had just vacated.

I narrowed my eyes at Che. He was a jaguar shifter. How had

he escaped my knowledge? "You, me. Over there. Now." I gestured toward a corner of the lobby.

Katya's eyes widened. "Carter, what's going on?"

"I just need to speak to him. I'll be right back."

She opened her mouth to protest, but I stormed over to the corner before she spoke.

Che joined me, his expression tight. "Who are you, and why are you in this hotel? Why are there suddenly so many jaguar shifters showing up?"

I clenched my fists. "Funny. I was going to ask you the same thing. How long have you been working here?"

He narrowed his eyes. "Since Jennifer and the twins moved here to open the hotel for business."

"Why did I never sense your presence?" I demanded. "You've been here for five years?"

"I don't have to tell you anything. Why are *you* here?"

"I've lived here my whole life! My family practically ran this town. Then *I* ran *them* out of town."

Che flinched. "You did? By yourself?"

"No. I'm part of a new family now."

"Those jokers I just kicked out?"

I rubbed a bruise on my face. "Hardly. I'm already trying to figure out how to run them out, too."

He studied me, his stance growing less threatening. "The reason you never sensed me is because I went to great lengths to cover my scent." He paused. "Clearly it's fading."

"I know about Katya."

"Figures."

"Did you know her dad?" I stared him down. "Is that why it's your job to make sure she remains safe?"

Che cracked his knuckles, but he finally gave a slight nod. "We were friends from opposing families, both tired of the old ways. Long story short, we both left our respective families. Mine didn't care, but his did. He'd fallen in love with Jennifer and she'd gotten pregnant. They were tracking him, and finally found him after the twins were born. Before he died, I promised to protect his family."

"And now they're here." I clenched my fists.

"Yeah."

I glanced back at Katya. She was watching us with interest. I turned back to Che. "You need to do something to cover up your scents."

"Clearly. Why do you care so much?"

"Hers is more prominent. For quite some time I was under the impression that there was a lone female jaguar shifter in the area. You know how dangerous that is."

He nodded. "If you sensed her, they probably did, too."

"And they think they own her. She has no clue she's a shifter, does she?"

"Only I know. Kevin never told Jennifer, although if you ask me, he should've. Now the twins don't know about her being a shifter, either."

"Why haven't you told them? Katya needs to know. One of these days, she's going to shift. You realize that, don't you? It's unavoidable. What if she's somewhere in public?"

"I promised Kevin."

I gave him a double-take. "What's more important? Keeping a promise to a dead guy or telling Katya that she could turn into a jaguar if she's not careful? I'm surprised it hasn't happened already."

"She's managed to stay a virgin. That helps. If Alley was the shifter, I'd have had to tell her long ago. But the way you and Katya are looking at each other, one of us is going to have to have the talk with her."

"I'm not that kind of guy. I just met her this morning."

"You sure seem to care about her."

"Because I've been searching for her for years. Maybe since she arrived. There's something about her that's easier to sense than you."

"It's because she hasn't shifted yet. The guy who sold me the spices to cover her scent warned me that might happen."

"Darrell."

"You know him?" Che scratched his chin.

"Yeah, I've been to the *spice shop*. I told you, I've lived here my whole life. And I know most of what he sells are magical concoctions."

We stared at each other for a few moments before Che finally spoke. "So, you're truly only here to protect Katya?"

"Yes. I've been worried for a long time about the lone female jaguar. It probably sounds strange, but I feel like it's made me closer to her somehow." I studied him. He didn't respond. "I'm glad she's not actually alone."

"Doesn't mean she's in any less danger. Those other shifters are from her family. They're not going to give up easily."

"Believe me, I've already figured that out." One of my ribs popped. I really needed to get out to the woods and turn.

Che arched a brow. "You need to shift?"

"Later. I promised Katya I'd go for a dip. You'll post yourself outside her door? My friends can help with that."

"No offense, but I'm not trusting werewolves to watch Katya."

I glared at him. "They're my family, and you might just have to trust them. And the others, too. Without their help, I'd never have run my father out of town."

He rubbed his chin, looking deep in thought. "No, I can't say I'll ever trust them, but I do trust you."

I gave a slight nod. "The feeling's mutual."

Che stepped closer. "Here's a deal for you. While you're swimming, I'll run over to Darrell's spice shop and convince him to come up with something a little stronger for Katya. Then you wait to shift until I return, and I'll stay outside her door. I want you to watch her while she's on campus. I have to stay here and work during the day."

I held out my hand. "Deal."

He grasped my hand, and we shook.

"You do realize that Katya would probably hate knowing that we're trying to protect her, especially making the plans behind her back."

Che glanced behind me. "I'm well aware of that, but unless you want to try and convince her that she's a jaguar shifter, we have no other choice."

"Oh, I know it. We're going to have to figure out a way to tell her so that she'll believe us."

"She doesn't even like watching or reading paranormal stuff. Alley's all over that. She wanted a vampire boyfriend for years. Katya? Not so much. She thinks that stuff is stupid."

I ran my fingers through my hair. "Looks like we have our work cut out for us."

Chapter Ten

Katya

FINALLY, CARTER AND CHE PARTED WAYS. CHE HEADED TO THE front desk and spoke with my mom. Carter came over to me and smiled, and it nearly melted me.

My heart raced. I wanted to be irritated at him for keeping me out of his conversation with Che, but he made it impossible. I was going to start acting like Alley before long if I kept hanging around him.

"Sorry that took so long," he said. "I just wanted to make sure the security around here is tight. Can't have any repeats of earlier."

"I appreciate the concern, but I'll be fine. Nothing like that has ever happened before, and those jerks are gone."

Carter's expression tightened. "Doesn't mean they won't come back."

His intensity sent a cold shiver down my body. I wasn't used to anyone being that concerned about me. Usually, guys saved that for Alley. But that was because they tended to find me intimidating— it was my curse.

"You ready to go swimming?" There was that smile again.

My breath caught, but I managed to find my voice. "Yeah. Let's go."

We walked side-by-side to the pool, and his arm kept brushing against mine. I wished I didn't have the kimono on because, thin as it was, it was keeping his skin from touching mine.

When we got there, everyone else was already in the pool. Our group had it to ourselves. Alley and her friends were chasing Carter's friends.

It struck me that I was the only one there who didn't have any friends with me. What if Carter realized that? Would he think there was something wrong with me? It wasn't like I didn't have any friends. They just weren't there in the pool. If I'd thought of it, I could've invited anyone on the volleyball team.

"Are you okay?" Carter's voice broke through my sudden insecurity.

I forced a smile. "Yeah, of course. Guess I'm more shaken up than I thought."

He frowned.

No, don't frown. Come back to me, smile.

I smiled wider. "But I'm okay. Let's jump in."

"Sounds good to me." He reached for the hem of his shirt and pulled it up, slowly revealing his perfect torso.

My mouth dropped and I tried not to stare, but I couldn't help it. At least I wasn't drooling.

He pulled the shirt over his head, and I quickly turned away. I needed to get ahold of myself. Quickly. I untied my kimono and laid it on the lounge chair where he'd tossed his shirt.

Carter nodded toward the deep end. "Ready?"

I nodded. How could I talk around him when he only wore shorts?

"I'll race you."

"Okay." My voice was so quiet, I wasn't sure he could actually hear it.

He turned toward the water, sprinted over, and dove in. Every move he made was perfect. The whole beautiful thing appeared to be in slow motion, allowing me to savor it all.

Then I remembered we were supposed to race.

Everyone else was staring at me. As I stared at Carter.

I looked like such a fool. My face flamed for the billionth time that day. I ran over to the pool, and just before jumping in, I stumbled over something. There wasn't even anything there. But I fell forward nonetheless.

My arms flew out in opposing circular motions. My body smacked flat on the water. I belly-flopped in front of Carter, my sister, and their friends. After drooling over him like a pathetic lovesick puppy.

Water shot up my nose, into my mouth, and into my ears as I submerged. I spat the water out and struggled to recover so I could at least emerge with some grace.

Arms wrapped around me. Was Carter trying to help me out from my humiliating leap?

No. Whoever had me was pulling me down. Taking me away from the surface. Away from the air I desperately needed.

I struggled to get away, squirming and kicking. My arms were pinned against me, unable to move. I tried shouting, but only made bubbles. Water rushed around me as I descended.

I kicked and struggled all the harder. My lungs cried out for air. They burned. I had to get to the surface. Immediately.

The arms around me tightened. Together we went further down.

Why wasn't the other person struggling to breathe? He or she needed air too. Did they have an oxygen mask?

Hands gripped my arms. I struggled against them, but they pulled me up. My eyes focused. Carter was in front of me. He was trying to help.

I kicked the person pinning me all the harder. There wasn't much time before I passed out. My lungs were on fire. They would explode.

A rib popped. Then another. My muscles ached in a way they never had before, not even during my hardest workouts. Why was this happening again?

I felt myself moving upward. Fast. I broke to the surface, and gasped for air, unable to get any in quickly enough. Carter held me close, and I leaned against him, unable to keep myself upright. I couldn't get enough oxygen.

Somehow we made it to the side of the pool. He lifted me up, and I managed to sit on the side, still gasping for air.

Carter jumped up and put his arm around me. "What happened?"

Did he mean my super-cool belly-flop or one of our guests pulling me under? Not that it mattered, I still couldn't talk.

"Did you swallow water?"

I shook my head. It was a miracle I hadn't.

Everyone crowded around me, speaking at once. It made me dizzy—like I was being pulled under all over again.

"What happened?" Alley sat next to me, her eyes wide with fear. "Why didn't you come up?"

"Someone pulled me under!" I glared at her friends and Carter's. "Which one of you was it? That wasn't funny."

Alley's face paled. "It wasn't any of us. We were all over at the other end, diving for a dime."

I turned to Carter. He nodded. "It's true. When I surfaced, all I saw were bubbles. I thought you were going to come up but I realized you were going down. It was taking too long, so I went down after you and saw you struggling."

My stomach sank. "You didn't see the person pulling me?"

"You were alone, Katya."

"It was the spirit." Alley's face paled even more. She almost looked like a ghost herself.

"That's ridiculous," I snapped. Or was it? There was nobody else in the pool. Unless they were all pulling a fast one on me. "Which one of you was it? Just admit it."

Alley took my hand in both of hers. Tears shone in her eyes. "I swear to you, it was none of us."

I couldn't remember the last time I'd seen her so upset. She had to be telling the truth. I turned to Carter. His face was nearly as white as hers.

"Let's get you out of here." He helped me up.

"No, we came here to have fun. Let's swim."

Alley shook her head. "I'm not going back in there. That ghost came out before midnight and went after you. It isn't safe. We should probably tell Mom to close the pool for good."

"We can't do that. The pool is the one thing that makes us stand out among the other hotels. She'll lose business."

"Fine, but I'm going to insist she gets a lifeguard, then. One who isn't afraid of ghosts."

Everyone spoke over each other. I leaned against Carter, trying to block them out. He held me close, then we all grabbed our towels and headed upstairs.

Alley turned to me once we were outside of our rooms. "Now do you believe in the paranormal? You try so hard to deny anything you can't see, but now you've experienced it. You have to know it's real."

Everyone stared at me, waiting for a response. Was I the only sane one who didn't believe in ghosts? There had to be a logical explanation for what happened. I just didn't know what it was. There was always a good reason.

"My head hurts. I just need to rest." I unlocked my door.

"Did you swallow water?" Alley asked. "Should we get you to a doctor?"

"No." I glared at her. "I just need to lay down."

"Have you heard of dry drowning? If you start to feel sick, get me right away. I'll drive you to the ER."

"What the heck is dry drowning?"

"People die hours after swimming because they got water in their lungs and didn't realize it. What are the symptoms? Dizziness and fever, I think? A change in skin color? I can't remember. I'm going to look it up!" Alley pulled out her phone and slid her finger around her screen.

"I'm not going to drown in my bed." I sighed out of frustration. "It's not even a waterbed like Mom had when we were little."

"Here are the symptoms." She shoved the phone in my face and pointed. "Coughing, chest pain, trouble breathing, and exhaustion. Also, forgetfulness and irritability."

"I'm only irritated because you won't let me go in my room."

"Kat, I'm serious. If you have even one of those symptoms, you have to tell someone. I'm really scared."

I took a deep breath. "I don't have any, but if I do, you'll be the first person I tell. Okay?"

"What if you pass out and can't tell anyone?"

Carter cleared his throat. "I'll keep an eye on her. If she starts to act weird or has any of those symptoms, I'll drag her to see a doctor, even if she kicks and screams."

"You swear?"

"On my mother's grave."

"Your mom's dead?" Alley gave him a double-take.

"Yeah, and I swear on her grave that I'll keep Katya safe. That's how serious I am."

Alley seemed doubtful, but finally nodded. "Come and get me if she has *any* of the signs."

Carter nodded, then turned to his friends.

While everyone was talking, I slid into my room. I couldn't recall the last time Alley had been so worried about me. Maybe she was just afraid she'd lose me, and it had made her think of Dad. Neither of us wanted our family to shrink more than it already had.

I grabbed some clothes from my closet and hurried into my bathroom, locking the door behind me. In all the commotion, I'd forgotten to grab my kimono. Not that I cared. I couldn't imagine going swimming ever again after what I'd just gone through.

I pulled off my suit, hung it on the shower rod, then reached for my dry clothes, but the smell of chlorine on my skin and hair stung my nose. I needed a shower. Maybe that would help me forget everything.

Unless someone tried to drown me in the shower. It wasn't impossible. An invisible person had pulled me under in the pool. Who was to say that same person hadn't followed me up to my room?

Ugh. Now Alley and all her superstitions were getting to me. There were no ghosts or other creatures of the night. Those were just stories people told to scare each other.

I turned on the shower as hot as I could stand it and showered off, soaping myself three times until I was certain I'd gotten rid of all the chlorine.

By the time I was done in the bathroom, my hair had air dried. Wearing a pair of my least-revealing pajamas, I came out and saw Carter standing near my bed, staring out the window. He still wore only his damp shorts and had a folded towel across his shoulders.

I studied his back. It was just as perfect as his front. I wanted to reach out and feel to see if it was as tight as it looked. What was going on with me? I cleared my throat, trying to distract myself.

He turned around. Oh, heavens. That physique. I held his gaze, trying to forget about the rest of him. It didn't work.

"How do you feel?"

Like kissing the barely-dressed guy standing next to my bed. My face heated again. "Better."

"No dry-drowning symptoms?"

"Other than irritation at my twin? Nope."

The corners of his mouth twitched. "She cares about you. I think it's sweet."

I shrugged. "You can call it sweet. I still say it's annoying."

"Family that truly cares can be hard to come by. Try to appreciate it."

I studied him, trying to imagine what he'd gone through that would make him say that. Maybe the loss of his mom?

He scratched his arm, right next to one of his tattoos. "Mind if I get a shower?"

"Go ahead."

Carter headed into the bathroom. Just before closing the door, he turned back to me. "Oh, I ordered pizza. Thought you might be hungry."

Maybe he was the world's most perfect guy.

Chapter Eleven

Carter

I RUBBED FRUITY SHAMPOO IN MY HAIR AND TRIED TO MAKE sense of Katya's near-drowning. I'd never heard of a ghost changing an MO so drastically, so I had a hard time believing the famed spirit had gone after Katya.

As I rinsed the shampoo, an idea struck me. What if she had actually started to shift under water? Being pulled under by a ghost might have been the only thing that made sense to her. And honestly, a failed shift was the only thing that made any real sense.

The good news was that she *hadn't* shifted. I drew in a deep breath and tried to take solace in that fact. I finished the shower and smelled like citrusy body wash and fruity shampoo. At least it beat smelling like chlorine.

I dried my hair with a purple-flowered towel and raked my fingers through my hair since I didn't have a comb with me. I lifted my arms and sniffed my pits. They were okay for now, but I still needed deodorant. I glanced around the bathroom. There was some exotic orchid scented antiperspirant.

That was where I drew the line. I'd rather risk sweating than smelling like a flower—that was far worse than fruity. If either Alex or Bobby caught a whiff of that, I'd never hear the end of it.

I double-checked my reflection before going into Katya's room. She sat on the bed, with the extra-large pizza box open, already eating.

"Sorry. I was too hungry to wait."

"That's why I got it." I sat on the other side of the box, grabbed the biggest piece, and dug in. With that first bite, I realized just how hungry I was, too.

We ate in silence, and I contemplated the day's events. What a day it had been. Not only had I found her after so much searching, but I had learned so much about her. And then I ran into other jaguar shifters. I hadn't seen another one in so long.

I glanced over at her as she picked up another slice. Between the two of us, we'd easily finish the entire pizza. I studied her, trying not to be obvious. Her coloring and breathing both seemed fine. That was a relief, but I wasn't letting her out of my sight just yet.

She finished off her piece, then leaned back against her pillows. "Sorry I'm not more talkative."

I met her gaze and smiled. "Don't apologize. This is nice, even without conversation."

Katya nodded and closed her eyes. "It is."

"How are you feeling?"

"Better, now that I've eaten."

I closed the pizza box and moved it out of the way, giving her more room to stretch out, which she did. She was beautiful even when almost asleep. It was so hard not to kiss her. It felt like we'd known each other much longer than we had. I supposed waiting so long to find her made me feel like that.

"Do you need anything?" I asked.

"Just sleep—and not because I'm exhausted from dry drowning symptoms. It's been a long day and I'm tired."

"I believe you." I pulled the covers out and covered her after she climbed under. "Sweet dreams."

She opened one eye. "Are you real?"

"Of course."

Katya mumbled something I couldn't understand and closed her eyes. I brushed some hair away from her face and gently pressed the back of my fingers along her cheek and forehead. She didn't feel feverish or chilled.

"I'm fine."

I smiled. "Yes, you are." In many more ways than one.

Her breathing deepened almost right away. My bones ached, demanding to shift soon. I ignored them, not wanting to leave her side. Not when she had a pack of jaguar shifters who wanted to steal her away, and not when she'd just suffered not one but two attacks in a row. Then there was the whole dry drowning thing— just one more thing to worry about.

I turned off the light, pulled up her desk chair, and sat down just a few feet from her. The rhythmic sounds of her breathing lulled me into wanting to sleep. I closed my eyes, listening for anything that could be wrong.

Knock, knock.

I pulled myself out of sleep and checked my phone. It had been two hours. I stretched, then felt Katya's forehead again before answering the door.

Che stood there. "How's she doing?"

"Sleeping like a baby. I was just sitting on a chair." I didn't know why I felt like adding the last part.

"Nobody tried to get in?"

I shook my head. "Nope."

"Good. Okay, I'll stay by the door all night and make sure nobody tries to get in. Then you'll head over around the time she leaves for classes?"

"Yeah. I can have my friends watch the door and give you a break."

He grimaced. "I don't trust werewolves."

I stepped into the hallway and closed the door behind me. "Let's not talk shifters within her hearing."

"She's asleep."

"People wake up." I glanced up and down the hall to make sure nobody was around. "So, what you're saying is that you'd rather stand guard all night than let someone give you a break?"

His expression stiffened. "No, what I'm saying is that I trust myself to watch over her more than I trust werewolves watching over her."

"I told you, they're my family. I trust them to watch her."

Che stood taller. "I'm not going anywhere."

"Okay, just know that I want her safe."

"I appreciate the help, I do. Just not from werewolves. I trust you—you're a jaguar who also left the traditional families. We have to stick together."

I nodded. "That's actually how my pack runs, though it extends beyond shifters. You'd be surprised. We even have a vampire."

"In a werewolf pack?"

"Right."

"And he doesn't fear for his life?"

"No, *she* doesn't."

Che studied me. "You've struck my curiosity. I want to hear more about that later. Go and shift. Meet me here about eight."

"Will do. Last chance to get help from my friends."

He folded his arms and shook his head. "Maybe some other time, after I get to know them. For now, no."

"Okay."

I headed to the room I'd rented and filled Bobby and Alex in on everything, asking them to check on Katya every so often. What if the other jaguars came back and overpowered Che? He might have been willing to risk it, but I wasn't.

"Hey, you smell nice," Bobby teased as I left.

There was no hiding anything from shifters. Not with our hypersensitive sense of smell.

I ignored him and hurried out of the building and across the street to where I'd parked my car that morning. It felt like days ago.

As I drove home, my muscles burned and various bones popped. I gritted my teeth and clutched the steering wheel, fighting the shift. Only a few more minutes until I reached the woods.

Once parked, I scrambled from my car and undressed, putting my clothes inside. Then I closed my eyes and shifted almost immediately. It was so fast, I barely felt anything.

I opened my eyes, and everything was brighter and more vivid with my jaguar sight. The scents of the forest all grew stronger around me. I walked toward the forest and roared, the sound echoing and warning any potential threats to stay away.

Without another thought, I burst into a run and raced into the trees. Luckily the Olympic National Park gave me far more miles than I would need to burn off my energy. I tore through the familiar area, barely taking in the scenery around me.

After a while, I came to a stream and paused. It was full of fish, which I loved catching as a jaguar. I easily snatched up the first few—there were so many, it was hardly a challenge. Then after eating those fish, I played with the next couple before finally feeling full.

I padded around, enjoying the pleasant silence. There was nothing like the solitude of the forest, and as a jaguar, it couldn't be better.

As my stomach settled, my mind wandered back to Katya and all the issues I needed to deal with as a human. I jogged toward the Faeble, Tap's supernatural bar in the middle of the woods. He was a former troll king and had more resources than almost anyone I knew. If someone knew about the new jaguars in town, it would be him.

Once there, I went around to the back where shifters kept extra clothes in cubbies. After making sure nobody was around, I turned back into a human and got dressed.

Inside, glass shattered followed by roars of laughter. There were several groups who liked to give Tap trouble, and I never could figure out why he put up with them.

There was a chance he might be too busy to talk with me, but I would try. Inside, a group of mesmers filled a banquet room, laughing like lunatics.

"What are you looking at, jaguar?"

A full glass of brown liquid flew toward my head. I ducked out of the way just before it shattered against the wall, then I headed over to the bar. Tap and Quinn were busy mixing drinks and didn't see me sit at one of the stools.

"What's up with the mesmers?" I asked.

Quinn glanced over and wiped sweat from his brow. "It's one of their top leader's birthdays. They're extra crazy."

"Why do you put up with all that?"

"We have a deal." Tap filled a tray with drinks of every color and raced toward the party room.

I leaned over the bar and looked at Quinn, who was busy wiping the counter. "I can't imagine what they have to offer."

"You'd be surprised." He threw the towel into the sink. "What can I get you?"

"Nothing to drink. Can you take a break?" I nodded toward the back door. "I have some questions."

"Yeah, sure. If it's quick."

"Should be."

We headed out back. Quinn waved at Tap, letting him know he was taking a break. One of the mesmers picked up Tap and threw him into the air.

"What the—?"

Quinn pulled me away. "He can handle himself."

"Are you sure?"

"Yeah, don't worry about him." Once outside, Quinn pulled out a cigarette. "Want one?"

I shook my head.

He lit it and turned to me. "So, what do you want to know?"

"Know anything about jaguar shifters coming to town?"

"No, we've been pretty busy with those mesmers. This is the third straight day of that party." Quinn blew a smoke ring.

I stared at him. "A three-day party?"

"Nobody can celebrate like those tricksters."

"Apparently. So, no jaguars have come into the Faeble?"

"Not other than you."

I leaned against the building and tapped my foot. "Haven't heard anything?"

"Nope." He blew another smoke ring. "Why? Does it have anything to do with that girl you're tracking?"

"Yeah, actually. I finally found her, and the same exact day, so did her family of origin—only she doesn't know she's a shifter. No idea about our world."

Quinn arched a brow. "So she thinks she's just a human? And those traditional jags want to pull her into their backward lifestyle?"

"Exactly."

"Well, I can keep an ear out. Maybe some patrons will talk about them. What do you want to know, specifically?"

I sighed, frustrated. "Anything. I don't know where they're from, how long they've been searching for her, or anything. One thinks she's his bride-to-be and that he owns her."

"Typical." Another smoke ring. "Do you want me to ask Tap about them? Might not be for a couple days. I don't know how long the mesmers plan on staying."

"I hope they pay well."

"You have no idea."

I studied him, but he didn't give me any indication of what he meant. We stood in silence for a while, and I tried to think of any other questions to ask. It was hard to think. My eyes were growing heavy.

Quinn dropped his cigarette and smashed it. "Anything else you need? I gotta get back in there."

Glass shattered inside as though to prove his point.

"No. Just call me if you learn anything. Anything at all."

"Will do." He nodded and went inside just as more laughter erupted.

I headed over to the cubbies and undressed before shifting and running back home. After changing back into my clothes, I headed inside to see if anyone was awake.

As soon as I opened the door, the hearty aroma of stew greeted me from the pack's dinner earlier. Laura, our pack mother, made the best food for us every night.

The house was quiet, so I crept into the kitchen and warmed up leftovers. Despite the pizza earlier, two shifts left me famished.

As I was finishing up, Toby meandered in. He gave me a double-take. "I thought you were staying in the hotel?"

"I needed to shift."

He nodded knowingly and sat across from me. "How are things going with Katya? I still can't believe she's the jaguar you've been searching for. I was talking about that with the rest of the pack, and we're all shocked. It even turns out Elsie is in art with her, and she never picked up any supernatural vibes, either."

"You have Darrell to thank for that. Katya has a bodyguard, and he's been covering their scents."

"That makes sense. She's done an excellent job of hiding."

"It's easy for her since she has no clue."

We sat in silence until Toby finally spoke. "What are you going to do now?"

I filled him in on everything that had happened since I saw him on campus earlier.

Toby released a long, slow breath. "Sounds like we might have another battle on our hands."

"I'm hoping it doesn't come down to that. Che and I were able to handle them tonight."

"You don't think they'll show up with more of their family?" He arched a brow.

I frowned. "I'm sure they will."

"I'm waiting to hear back from Gessilyn to see what she or one of the other witches can dig up. Maybe you should get some sleep. You look exhausted."

Irritation built in my gut. It always did when Toby tried to tell me what to do, even when he was right. I nodded, though, and stood.

"And I'll let you know when I hear back from Gessilyn."

We said our goodbyes, then I made my way back to the hotel. I was tired enough that I could've fallen asleep walking.

Before heading to my room, I went over to check on Katya's hall.

Che wasn't next to her door. Or in front of it. Or anywhere.

My throat nearly closed up. I raced over to the door and looked around frantically.

Che stood down the hall, speaking on his phone. He waved when he saw me.

Relief washed through me, and I very nearly collapsed. I took a deep breath and headed back to my room.

Bobby snored from one bed and Alex sat on a chair. He glanced up from his phone when I walked in. "I just checked on her. That jaguar wasn't too happy to see me."

"Thanks." I fell on top of the empty bed.

"Any news?"

"Nothing worth mentioning." I closed my eyes and fell right to sleep.

Chapter Twelve

Katya

THE NEXT COUPLE WEEKS FLEW BY IN A BLUR OF VOLLEYBALL practices and games, classes and homework, and barely any sleep. Carter was around a lot. We talked over homework, and he cheered me on when I played volleyball.

Neither of us mentioned my near-drowning or the jerks who tried to attack me. We just got to know each other more, and I was pleased that he was far more than just a good-looking guy. He had a lot of depth and a great sense of humor.

The more time I spent with him, the more I wanted. If he didn't go with me to the games and practices or to the library, I wouldn't have gotten much time with him other than running into him on campus. Though I honestly wondered if that wasn't on purpose, too.

"Are you ready for the final game?" His voice brought me back to the present.

I glanced up from my math problem and smiled at him. It was

nearly impossible not to. Just looking at him overwhelmed me. "I hope so."

"You are." He put his hand on top of mine and squeezed. "Your entire team is. I've seen you guys, and you're getting better each day."

He was right. We'd beaten other teams each time in the play-offs, and with each new win, our confidence grew by leaps and bounds. But even so, the team we were going to face the next evening was undefeated.

I realized Carter was talking again, so I stared into his gorgeous eyes, still unable to focus on what he was saying. Even though he'd been my constant companion for two weeks, it was still hard to believe he probably had feelings for me. We hadn't talked about them, but things like his hand lingering on mine and spending all his free time with me spoke volumes.

It also sent my heart racing so fast I feared him hearing it.

Carter's phone rang. He squeezed my hand. "I've got to take this. Be right back."

"Okay."

Don't be too long.

Why couldn't I say things like that to him?

He flashed his pearly whites, then headed toward the library stairs. I turned back to my math homework.

A few minutes later, someone sat next to me, not across from me as Carter had been. I glanced up and saw Paige from the volley-ball team.

"Not with Carter?" She arched a brow.

"He's on the phone."

"And you guys are still just friends?" She made air quotes when she said *just friends*.

"Yes."

"Really? I've seen the way you guys look at each other. I'd have staked my claim weeks ago."

"I only met him two weeks ago. Well, actually two weeks and two days."

She grinned. "You *are* in love."

I looked around. "Shh! Don't say that so loud."

"You afraid he's going to hear?"

My face burned. "Maybe."

"Why? He obviously feels the same for you, and seriously, he's got to be the hottest guy on campus."

My face heated even more. "Can we talk about something else?"

"You're so cute, it's like—" Her eyes widened. "Wait. Is he your first love?"

"Again, can you keep your voice down? Seriously."

"He is! How did you make it to college without—?"

"Because I was focused on my grades. I was more interested in getting scholarships than I was in finding a boyfriend."

"Well, don't be too slow in snatching him up. I can think of several other girls who have their eyes set on him."

Jealousy ran through me. A rib popped. That hadn't happened since the night those two guys cornered me.

Paige gave me a funny look. "What was that all about?"

"Just my back." I stretched it.

"Maybe you should see a chiropractor."

"After the final game."

"Well, I wouldn't wait. That sounded painful."

It really was.

"Oh, here comes Carter. I'll leave you two lovebirds alone. See you at practice." She winked and hurried off.

Carter came over, his expression strained.

"Is everything okay?"

"Yeah, it's fine." He sat down, not looking at me.

"What's the matter?"

"Nothing. Are you ready for dinner? You won't want to go to practice hungry."

Practice was at five, so if I ate first, it'd have to be a really early dinner. But that wasn't the point. Something was clearly wrong, but he was trying to act like it wasn't.

I put my hand on top of his. "What's wrong?"

"Nothing I want you worrying about. You have enough on your plate."

"Why won't you tell me?" I stared at him until he finally looked at me.

"Like I said, I don't want you worrying. Che and I have it covered."

"Che?" If I was Carter's love interest, then Che was his new best friend. It was kind of weird, because Che was the closest thing to a father figure I'd ever had. If anyone was going to walk me down the aisle someday, it would be him.

"All you need to worry about is your homework and finals."

If I'd had feathers, they'd have been ruffled. Irritation shoved aside all my loving feelings. "Carter, just tell me what's going on. I'm not some weakling you have to protect."

"I never thought—"

"Yes, you did. Otherwise, you wouldn't be concerned about upsetting poor, defenseless me."

"Katya, you're taking this all wrong."

"Am I?" I packed my things into my tote bag.

"Yes. That's not how I meant it at all. I just don't want to add unnecessary stress on top of everything else you're dealing with."

I glared at him. "If you trusted me, you'd just tell me. I'll have dinner on my own, thank you very much."

He rose, practically knocking over his chair. "Wait."

Tears threatened. I turned before he could see how upset I was. All these raging emotions I'd had lately were driving me crazy. I wasn't a crier. I was the tough twin. "I'll see you later. Have fun with Che."

"Katya—"

A bone popped somewhere, but I was too upset to tell which one. I hurried toward the stairs, eager to get away from him.

It was like he didn't know me at all after spending practically every waking hour with me. Did he really think I was a weak little princess who couldn't handle anything? Hadn't he seen me fighting those two jerks? What about how aggressive I'd been in the volley-ball playoffs?

Once out of the library, I darted down a path that went behind the building in hopes he'd think I'd gone toward the cafeteria or deli.

I made it to the arts building and watched some ballerinas until I calmed down enough to realize how hungry I was. Keeping a lookout for Carter, I grabbed a bite to eat and then headed to the gym for practice.

At first, I was glad he wasn't there, but then a wave of disappointment washed through me.

"Come warm up," the coach called.

I put all of my raging emotions into volleyball and ignored the occasional popping bone. It was probably just a side effect of working my body so hard. Everything would settle back down after the game the next day.

Near the end of practice, just as I was about to serve the ball, Carter walked into the gym. His face was bruised and blood dripped down from the corner of his mouth.

My arm froze mid-serve. The ball flopped to the ground halfway before it reached the net. My coach and teammates yelled at me, but I barely took notice of them.

Carter waved for me to go back to the game. I managed to finish the rest of the practice without any more mishaps, but I couldn't stop thinking about him. What had happened?

After practice was finally over, I rushed over to him and studied his wounds close up. His lower lip was split and caked in dried blood, and he had several bruises around his face, including around his right eye and on his chin. I traced the one on his chin with my thumb. "What happened? Will you finally tell me what's going on?"

"Yeah. Let's get out of here first."

"Okay." I grabbed my things, and we walked toward the hotel. Though the air was warm, I shivered.

Carter put his arm around me and took a deep breath. "Those guys from a couple weeks ago are back."

I turned to him. "What?"

"Those guys who tried to attack you."

"I know who you're talking about. They're back?"

"Yeah. I'm not sure they ever left, actually."

My stomach twisted in knots. "What do they want? Why did they hurt you?"

"Let's get you to the hotel."

I stopped walking. "No. I need you to tell me what's going on. Now."

"I will. I'll tell you everything, but not here. Not where others can overhear."

"Is it that bad?"

He gave a slight nod. "Let's go."

One of my ribs popped.

Carter's eyes widened.

"My back's been giving me issues. I'm going to see the chiropractor after tomorrow's game."

"Has that been happening? Your bones popping?"

"Yeah. I'm fine."

Color drained from his face. "It's worse than I thought."

"What is?"

"Everything. Come on."

How could my rib issue worry him so much? "What do you know?"

"Like I said, we need to discuss this. In private."

"Have I ever told you how much you annoy me?"

The corners of his mouth twitched. "No, but I can see it in your eyes sometimes."

"And you think that's funny?"

"Not at all." He kissed my forehead.

His lips on my skin sent a wave of pleasant emotions through me. I took a deep breath to regain my focus. "Don't try to distract me."

"I'm not trying to."

Trying or not, he was succeeding. I walked ahead of him, eager to get to the hotel and find out what was going on.

Carter walked alongside me, and we stayed quiet until we reached my home. We waved to my mom, who was busy checking a family in. In the hall leading to my room, we passed Che.

He had bruises on his face.

I froze in my tracks and glared at him. "What's going on? Did you two get into a fight?"

Carter put his arm around me. "We have to tell her everything. Now."

Che nodded. "I always knew this day was coming." His tone held sadness.

"What are you talking about?"

"You two should come to my room. I don't want to risk your mom or sister hearing us."

My stomach was such a mess of tight knots, I wasn't sure it could ever untangle itself. A rib popped, and then my hip. I cried out. They'd never been that painful before.

"Hurry." Carter glared at Che. "Before she shifts."

"Before I what?" I exclaimed.

They pulled me down the hall.

Chapter Thirteen

Carter

CHE'S ROOM WASN'T FAR FROM KATYA'S, BUT IT WAS DOWN THE hall farther, past a noisy laundry room. There were no other residences besides his. That made it unlikely anyone would overhear us. It was the perfect place to explain Katya's true nature to her.

And it was definitely time. Just as we walked to Che's room, her bones popped several more times. She cried out in pain each time.

I exchanged worried glances with Che. It might not be long before she shifted.

He unlocked his door and waved us inside, leading us to a small dining room. We sat at the table and Katya glared at us. "Now will you two tell me what's going on?"

"We'll tell you everything." I put my hand on top of hers and met her gaze. "Do you promise to keep an open mind?"

"Can you make this stop hurting?" Her voice was pinched.

I nodded. "We can. All the popping will stop, guaranteed." But the one thing I couldn't promise was that she'd like the answer—

shifting into a jaguar. I took a deep breath and tried to figure out the best place to start.

Che cleared his throat. "You know how you've always felt different from your mom and sister?"

Katya stared at him. "How did you know?"

"And you know how we've always had a connection?"

She swallowed, but didn't say anything.

"Well, there's a really good reason for that."

"I always thought it was because you were a father figure. And that you knew my dad. You've been willing to tell me more about him than Mom is."

"And what I'm about to tell you is something not even she knows about him."

Katya rubbed her side. Then she turned to me. "And you're somehow involved in this? With whatever's between Che and my dad?"

"I never knew your dad, but yeah."

She stared back and forth between the two of us. "And that'll explain why you two have become besties?"

I nodded yes. "Not that we'd call each other besties."

Katya rubbed her neck, closed her eyes, and took a deep breath. "Okay. Lay it on me. Why does this pain make me different from Mom and Alley?"

Che rubbed his own neck, but for entirely different reasons. "There's a family secret. It's so important that, even though your dad walked away from the family, he couldn't tell your mom. But you have to know now, because you've inherited it."

Katya's eyes flew open. "What have I inherited? Is it a disease? Is that what really killed him? Am I going to die, too?"

I placed my palm on her back. "You're perfectly healthy. I swear."

She turned to me, her expression panic-stricken. "What is it, then?"

I glanced over at Che. "Would it be better to just let her experience it? To see it? We could take her out to the forest."

Katya's face paled. "See what? Just tell me!"

My mind raced. I'd grown up knowing that one day I would shift. It was a rite of passage I'd eagerly awaited for years. I couldn't even remember anyone ever telling me. By the time I was old enough to speak, I just knew it as reality. "You'll keep an open mind?"

"I don't have much of a choice, now do I?" Another bone popped. She cried out.

I pulled her close, and turned to Che. "We need to get her out of here."

"Can we get to the woods in time? I don't have a car."

"I do."

Katya jumped up from her chair, tears shining in her eyes. "I'm not going anywhere until you two explain everything to me!"

I rose and met her gaze. "You're about to shift into a jaguar."

Her face paled even more, which I hadn't thought possible. "What?"

"Shifters are real." I took her hand, which shook in mine. "Werewolves, dragons, bears, and plenty more. You, me, Che—we're all jaguar shifters."

Katya turned to Che.

He nodded. "So was your dad, and so are those guys who attacked you that night you brought Carter here."

She swayed back and forth.

I pulled her close and held her, rubbing her back. "They're the reason Che and I are bruised and bloody. He called me when they showed up at the hotel again. I came over, and we had to fight them to leave."

"Wh-what do they want?"

Che and I exchanged another look. Katya might just fall completely apart if she knew they wanted her.

"Don't worry about them," I whispered.

She pulled out of my grasp and glared at me. "Don't tell me not to worry! What do they want? Those... those shifters?"

"You really want the truth?"

"That's all I've wanted all along."

"You." I let the lone word sink in.

Katya sat back down. "They want me?"

I nodded.

"Why?"

I didn't have the heart to tell her more.

She turned to Che. "Why?"

He frowned. "They're from your dad's family."

"They're my relatives?"

"Right."

"Like cousins or something?"

"Something like that." Che reached across the table and took her hand. "But you need to understand that there's a good reason your dad left them. He risked his life when he made that choice."

Katya's mouth fell open.

"Leaving put a target on his back. But mating with a human, that was like painting targets all over his body. That's what got him killed."

"Those people—they're the ones who killed my dad?" Katya shook.

Che nodded.

"They need to go to jail! Why are they walking around free?"

"Because shifters live by an entirely different set of rules and regulations. According to their laws, your father's death was justified."

"Because he walked away from them? Because he loved Mom?"

"Right."

She slunk into the chair. "This is too much."

I glanced at Che. "Should we take her out to shift?"

"The popping has stopped," she whispered. "And you don't have to talk about me like I'm not here."

"Sorry. What should we do?"

"Talk to me like I *am* here."

I brushed some hair away from her face. "No. I mean, do you

want to shift? Do you need something else?" I tried to imagine myself in her place, but couldn't.

"I just want to lie down. In my own bed."

Che threw me a worried glance before turning to her. "But what if you have to shift?"

Katya drew in a deep breath. "That passed. Nothing's popping, nothing's sore. I barely have the energy to walk to my room."

"I'll help you. Lean on me." I helped her to stand. The three of us trudged to her room. Che unlocked the door, and I helped Katya to her bed.

She sat and looked over at Che, then me. "What now?"

"Rest, if that's what you need," he said. "I'll be close."

Katya turned to me. "Will you stay?"

"Of course."

"Call me if you need anything," Che said.

I nodded. "And you let me know if those jaguars show up again."

"I doubt they will. At least not tonight. But if they do, you'll be the first to know."

"Oh, and Toby's sending over a couple of our pack members. Make sure they get a room close to here."

"Will do." He turned to Katya. "Do you need anything before I go?"

She shook her head.

He spun around and left, closing the door behind him.

I pulled the covers back, and Katya climbed underneath. After turning off the lights, I sat in a recliner.

"Hold me."

My pulse raced at the thought of climbing under the covers with her, but who was I to argue with what she wanted? I went around to the other side of the bed, kicked off my shoes, and slid over next to her, pulling her close. I tried to ignore how delicious she smelled and how soft her skin was.

We lay in silence for some time. She shook, drew in deep breaths, and every once in a while, drew even closer to me. I kissed the back of her head several times and threaded my fingers through hers. Not once did any of her bones pop.

"Is Professor Foley a jaguar shifter too?"

"Toby? No, he's a werewolf. Most of my pack is."

"Why do you live with them?"

"Because they're a helluva lot nicer than my family."

"So, when you say family, do mean pack? Or do you mean your literal family?"

"Jaguars hate the term pack. Most of our kind looks down on werewolves, so we use the term *family* loosely."

She nodded and took a deep breath. "Most of our kind are jerks?"

"That's putting it politely."

"Why does my dad's pack want me? Do they want me dead?"

My breath caught. The truth would likely gut her.

"I can handle the truth. I know I seem weak right now, but this is a lot to take in."

"You're anything but weak. I can't imagine how I'd handle hearing the news like you did, with no idea about the supernatural world."

"Supernatural world?"

I cringed. Why had I said that? The last thing she needed was more dumped on her plate.

"Tell me."

"Okay. There's a lot more than the various shifters out there. We're just a small part of the overall world of creatures that humans think only exist in stories and movies."

Katya took a deep breath. "You'll have to tell me about that later."

Relief washed through me. "For sure."

"So, am I now sworn to secrecy? I can't tell my twin about any of this?"

"No, it's far too dangerous."

"For her, or us?"

"Both."

We lay in silence again for a while. Then Katya rolled over and looked into my eyes. "What's going to happen when I shift?"

"It'll be like the popping you felt, only all over."

"In other words, it'll hurt."

"Yeah, especially at first, but it does get better."

"Does it always hurt?"

I took a deep breath. "Yeah, but it's manageable after a while. Once it's over, you'll forget all about it."

She grabbed my hand and pressed her palm against mine. It was a simple action, but it sent a wave of warmth through me. "What's it like, being a jaguar?"

"It's unbelievable. There's nothing that compares to running free and sensing everything so much more. It's hard to describe. Everything is brighter. The smells stronger. Noises crisper. Tastes are magnified. And the speed... we can't move nearly as fast in this state."

"It sounds amazing."

"It really is."

She threaded her fingers through mine. "Will you go with me when I shift?"

"Of course I will."

"Can we go now?"

I gave her a double-take. "Do you feel like you need to?"

"No, but now I'm curious."

"Then let's wait." I kissed her nose. "You've got the biggest game of the season tomorrow. If you're out all night running as a jaguar, you're likely to be exhausted."

"What if my bones start popping and cracking again?"

"You've held off this long. One more day shouldn't be too difficult."

She looked deep in thought. "Why does my dad's family want me? I still don't understand. Do they want me dead because my dad left them?"

Anger raced through me as I thought of their motives. "No. Quite the opposite, actually. They want to bring you in."

Her mouth dropped open. "They accept me? They want to get to know me?"

It took all my self-control to keep my voice steady. "They want to possess you. To marry you to a man who will treat you like his property. You'd be nothing more than a maid and baby-making factory."

"You've got to be kidding. In this day and age?"

"Now you see why your dad left. Why Che left his family. Why I fought to be free of mine. I can't live under those archaic rules."

Katya was quiet for a moment. "Is it crazy that I'm more surprised by that than the fact that my body wants to turn into a jaguar?"

I traced her jawline with my thumb and scooted closer. "Not at all. The traditional ways make me sick. I would never treat anyone the way jaguar men treat females."

She pressed her soft, sweet lips on mine. My eyes widened with shock. Katya placed her palms on my face and kissed me hungrily.

I wrapped my arms around her and returned the kiss, following her lead. I didn't want to go faster than she did, especially given her emotional state. Having her mouth against mine sent a wave of excitement through me like I'd never experienced. I'd finally met the woman I was meant to be with.

She pulled away and leaned against the pillow, her eyes closed. "Thank you for telling me the truth."

I pulled her close and kissed her cheek. "You deserve nothing less."

A few moments later, her breathing deepened. Once I was sure she was asleep, I closed my eyes, too.

Chapter Fourteen

Katya

"EARTH TO KATYA." JESSIE'S VOICE BROUGHT ME BACK TO THE present.

We were halfway through the final game of the season. The game that would determine whether our team was number one or number two. We were taking a break. The score was tied. And here I was daydreaming about having woken in Carter's arms.

I'd forgotten to set my alarm and missed math. Carter had given me a quick kiss before promising to talk to Professor Foley, who he swore would understand completely.

Not that I'd have cared either way. Waking up to see Carter sprawled out next to me had been worth any consequence that may have come my way.

"What's going on?" Jessie asked. "The volleyball almost hit you twice. You haven't been yourself lately, and today we have to focus."

"I know. I recovered and hit the ball over the net both times, remember? I'm fine. It's just nerves."

"Maybe grab an energy drink or something. We're all depending on you."

"You're right. I'm focused. From here on out, nothing's on my mind but winning."

Relief washed over her face. "You swear?"

"Yeah. I'm going to grab that drink." I jogged over to the vending machines, waving to the crowd where Carter sat with my mom and Che. Alley was with the cheer squad, doing a complicated routine to build the excitement of the crowd.

I picked out a cherry-flavored energy drink and downed it without stopping. Just after I tossed it into the recycle bin, voices caught my attention. Familiar voices.

A chill ran down my spine. They sounded exactly like my attackers. My family. The people who wanted to force me into a horrible marriage.

Because we were all jaguar shifters. A wave of disbelief ran through me. Would that ever sound normal?

"There she is!"

A rib popped. At least this time I knew why.

I glanced around. I was hidden by the sides of the bleachers and was on the opposite side of the concession stands.

Nobody would see me if my dad's family dragged me away. It was also too loud for anyone to hear me if I screamed.

The four guys stepped around the corner. Two of them were my attackers. One of them thought they owned me.

Probably the one ogling me.

The others were rolling up their sleeves like they were preparing for a fight. They knew I didn't want to go with them, and yet they were still going to try and take me.

I needed to run, but my feet were frozen on the floor.

They all glared at me, especially the ogler. He was currently staring at my legs. Suddenly, I felt self-conscious about the short shorts.

My heart thundered in my chest, and my mouth went dry. I tried swallowing, but it was futile.

It would only be a matter of moments before they were close enough to reach me. A rib popped, followed by a hip. A searing pain ran throughout my body, starting at the base of my neck and moving downward, spreading out to my limbs as it went.

I focused on them. They appeared more crisp and clear than anything I'd ever seen. In fact, even the lighting had changed.

Had I shifted?

I looked down. No, I was still me. But it was probably only a matter of time before I turned in front of everyone. And I had no idea what that was like.

Each of their steps echoed as they neared.

How could I hear that over the noise of the crowd?

That realization was enough to kick my feet into gear. I spun around and raced to the volleyball court—in front of everyone. Those jerks wouldn't dare try anything with a packed gym watching everything.

"Where'd you come from?" Lola asked.

"I just grabbed an energy drink."

"No, I mean it's like you appeared out of nowhere."

Blood drained from my face. "What do you mean?"

"You... you weren't here, then suddenly you were."

"Maybe you're the one who needs some caffeine." I gave her a playful shove, but I couldn't help wondering if she was right. What if I'd run too fast? Could my jaguar nature have taken over because I was scared?

The coach called us over for a huddle to get us in the mindset for the last half of the big game. I stayed on high alert. Those four guys peeked around the bleachers where I'd just been.

My heart raced again. It seemed unreal that they wanted to take me away so that I could be a slave-wife of the creep ogler, but I couldn't deny the feeling I got when they were around. It matched everything Carter and Che had told me.

Somehow I managed to push them out of my mind once we started playing. I laser-focused on the ball and took all my nervous energy out on it.

My team cheered for me, and so did the crowd. The excitement in the air fed into how well I was doing. Each time I hit the ball, it sailed through the air faster than I'd ever hit it before. It was like I had quickly growing abilities.

The second half of the game flew by, and our score kept going higher and higher, hardly seeming to pause. Our opposing team could barely keep up. They grumbled and complained, falling further behind.

Finally, the game was over. We'd won by leaps and bounds. We cheered, along with half the audience, then my team piled on top of me in celebration.

The award ceremony went by in a blur. It took me a moment to realize I'd been declared MVP of the game. Everything was surreal.

Once things calmed down, Alley came over to me, squealing with excitement. "I've never seen you play like that before! What changed?"

Guilt stung at me for not being able to tell her the truth. I made up some excuse about getting caught up in the excitement.

Alley threw her arms around me, obviously buying the story. "MVP! That's so awesome!"

My mom, Che, and Carter broke through the crowd, giving me more hugs and congratulations.

"This calls for a celebration." Mom beamed. "Let's head over to your favorite restaurant!"

One of my ribs popped.

Che's eyes widened. He turned to Mom. "Why don't we let her get cleaned up and have a chance to rest?" He put his hand on my shoulder. "Does dinner or lunch tomorrow sound good?"

I threw him my most grateful expression. "That sounds perfect." I rubbed my neck for extra effect. "Thank you guys so much for coming out. It means the world."

"You think I'd miss it?" Mom looked at me like I was crazy. "I got about two hundred pictures."

"You didn't." She knew how much I hated having my picture taken.

She pulled out her phone. "Two hundred and thirty-eight, to be exact."

I shook my head.

"Well, some of them are of Alley cheering, but most were of you. Today's your day."

I groaned. "Just don't put them on social media."

"You're no fun. Not even the best ones? Just for my friends. I won't tag you if you don't want."

I glared at Che. He was the one who taught her how to tag people in photos.

"Sorry," he mouthed. He didn't look sorry.

"Well?" Mom asked.

"Okay, just don't tag me."

"You can tag me in mine." Alley grinned. "I want to see them all."

We agreed on a time and place to eat the next day, then Mom and Che headed back to the hotel, and Alley rejoined her friends.

Carter draped his arms over my shoulders and gazed into my eyes. "Finally, I have you to myself. You did phenomenal, you know."

"Stop."

"I would, but I mean it. You deserved MVP."

"Those guys showed up at halftime."

Carter's grin faded. "What?"

"Those two from the hotel a couple weeks ago."

"I know who you meant. Where did you see them?"

"Over by the vending machines. They were definitely approaching me, but I ran back over to the court."

His expression pinched. "They dared to show up even after Che and I made it clear they needed to leave you alone?"

I studied his face. "Wait a minute. Come to think of it, neither of you have any of the bruises you had last night. Why not?"

"We heal quickly. Haven't you noticed that about yourself?"

I thought back to a time Mom had been sure I'd broken my leg, but the X-ray had barely shown a hairline fracture. One doctor had even said it was so slight it could've been something else.

"Maybe," I answered Carter.

He rubbed my shoulders. "How are you feeling? Still want to shift tonight?"

A mixture of terror and excitement ran through me. "I think so."

"You're not sure?"

My hip popped. "My body is. My mind isn't."

Carter laced his fingers through mine. "I'll be with you every step of the way. My first shift wasn't all that long ago. I still remember how nerve-wracking and confusing it was."

My pulse drummed in my ears, making it hard for me to hear him. Other than fearing the unknown and the thrill of all the popping coming to an end, I also felt a spark of something else. Relief?

Something inside urged me forward.

Carter kissed my cheek. "Let's go to my car, then I'll take you to the woods near campus. Think you can wait that long?"

"I hope so." We were a couple hours away from the ferry which would take us home. "I don't suppose we can teleport?"

He shook his head. "But I have some friends who do. I'll have to introduce you sometime."

I stared at him. "Are you serious?"

"Yeah. Come on. We have a long drive ahead of us."

"Oh, I'd better tell Paige that I won't be driving back with her."

A few minutes later, Carter and I walked hand-in-hand through the parking lot.

"Did you park on the far end?" I asked.

"Yeah, I usually do."

"Afraid of scratches?" I joked.

"Actually, yes." He led me to what appeared to be a red Ferrari. No other cars were by it.

"Is that yours?"

"The one good thing my dad gave me."

My mouth dropped open.

Carter remote-unlocked it and held open the passenger door for me. I climbed in, utterly in shock. I'd never been in anything so nice before.

What else didn't I know about him? And were all his other secrets just as surprising?

Chapter Fifteen

Katya

CARTER TURNED DOWN THE MUSIC AS HE DROVE UP A LONG winding dirt road in the woods.

"Where are we going?"

"We're going to park at my home, walk a short way into the woods, then shift."

My heart raced at the thought. What if I couldn't shift? Or if I got stuck as a jaguar? Or something went wrong and I ended up half-human and half-jaguar?

"Are you okay?"

I struggled to find my voice. "Can anything go wrong while shifting?"

"Like what?"

"Not shifting all the way? Or not returning back to normal? Or... I don't know. Anything at all?"

He rested his hand on my knee and gave a gentle squeeze. "It's going to go fine, other than hurting. But the pain is normal, and given how long you've put this off, it'll probably be quick."

"Okay." I wasn't sure the word came out audible.

We came to a gate, and behind it was a gorgeous sprawling fully-restored blue Victorian-era mansion.

"You live here?"

He pressed a button on his visor, and the gate opened. "It's not as impressive as your hotel, but yes, this is where I call home. It belongs to Toby."

My math professor lived *here*? If he could afford not only the home but the land around it, what was he doing teaching math? Just for the fun of it?

"Toby likes to keep the appearance of being like the humans," Carter said, as though hearing my thoughts. "That's why he teaches. Well, that and he loves math. He's a nerd like that." Carter parked between a Hummer and a Bentley.

I was out of place—way out of my element. No one in my family even owned a car. We walked everywhere because the hotel was in such a central location.

Carter cut the ignition and turned to me, taking a deep breath. "There's one more thing you need to know."

"What?"

"We have to disrobe before shifting. Turning while dressed will destroy our clothes. That's partly why I brought you here. There are female shifters in my pack if you'd be more comfortable. They're werewolves, but they know all about shifting. Usually, whenever possible, shifters turn separately—not in mixed company. But sometimes it can't be avoided."

"Oh." My voice caught in my throat. I hadn't even considered clothes.

"On the other hand, if you'd be more comfortable with me, I swear I'll keep my back turned the whole time. It's whatever you want."

My mind raced. I didn't really want to shift with people I didn't know, but I also hadn't expected to get naked with Carter, either. I'd never gone past kissing with any guy.

"Katya?"

I turned to him, but couldn't meet his gaze.

"I can introduce you to them. They're all really nice. There's Toby's wife, Victoria, and her mom and sister, and another were-wolf named Stella. She was born human and was turned a few years back. Maybe you'd be more comfortable with her."

Finally, I met his gaze. I swallowed then shook my head. "No, you've been the one with me every step of the way. I trust you."

He leaned over and pressed his mouth on mine, tasting of mint. His rugged, woodsy scent overwhelmed me. "I promise to be fully worthy of your trust."

We got out of the car and headed to the woods. After walking for about ten minutes, he stopped and turned to me.

My pulse raced so fast I could hardly breathe. Maybe this was a bad idea. A really bad idea. Or maybe it was all a joke. People don't turn into animals. It was scientifically impossible. Not improbable, but actually impossible. What if this was all a horrible joke?

Carter put his hand on my arm.

I jumped.

"Everything is going to be fine. I promise." He smiled reas-suringly.

I didn't feel any better.

"Once we're jaguars, you'll feel so great that you won't even remember how nervous you were. Being scared is normal. I was secretly terrified the first time I shifted."

"You were?"

He kissed my palm. "Don't tell anyone, but I nearly wet myself. I was with my dad, uncles, and cousins. They had all shifted hundreds of times before. Basically, they just wanted to watch and see if I'd handle it like a man. Nobody really explained what would happen. I was just entertainment for them. That was just part of the initiation into manhood."

"That's terrible."

Carter nodded. "Traditional jaguar shifters are. What you can expect is pain, like I said before. Our bones completely transform and fur slices through our skin. It can feel like fire because it's so fast. Your muscles will feel like they're being torn apart—they're not. But then once you're in jaguar form, all will be right with the world."

"Does turning back hurt as much?"

"I never usually remember. It isn't unusual to lie down to fall asleep, then to wake in my human form."

"Naked?" I exclaimed, horrified at the thought of accidentally being discovered like that.

He nodded. "That's why we leave changes of clothes in various places around the woods and behind the mansion. But I also shift fully awake and aware plenty of times. You'll be fine either way. I'll protect you, and I swear I'll be a perfect gentleman. No peeking, I give you my word."

A wave of confidence ran through me. I needed to take advantage of it. "Let's do this."

Carter squeezed my hand. "Just stick your clothes in a bush. We'll try to turn back near here."

I nodded, already feeling my confidence waning.

He turned around and pulled off his shirt.

We were really doing this.

Carter pulled off his belt.

I spun around, face flaming.

This was actually happening. My heart raced even faster than before. I shook so hard I could barely get my jersey off. Behind me came the sounds of him sliding off his jeans.

My mind raced, and my hands stumbled even more. I took a deep breath and focused only on removing my uniform. I folded it and set it on the ground. Wearing only my underwear, I turned to make sure he wasn't looking.

He wasn't. He also had nothing on.

I whipped back around and struggled with my bra clasp.

"How's it going over there?" Carter asked.

"A-almost done." I quickly stripped down and shoved the clothes inside a bush. "Now what?"

"Just focus on shifting. You can talk to your jaguar if she's nervous about coming out."

"She? Isn't it me?"

"Yeah, of course, but a lot of shifters find that it helps. The werewolves even refer to their wolf selves as their inner wolf."

I closed my eyes and whispered for my jaguar self to emerge. My bones popped and cracked. It started with my ribs and hips, but then moved all over—to my neck and knees and even the bones in my hands and feet.

The searing pain I'd felt back at the gymnasium returned. My muscles burned. If I didn't know better, I'd have thought I was actually being burned to death.

I screamed, unable to stay silent. The sounds echoed all around me. More cracking bones. It felt as though every bone was breaking in half. I cried out again—if I had even stopped yelling in the first place.

Carter said something, but I couldn't understand him over my hollering. Hopefully, he wasn't telling me to be quiet. That wasn't possible.

I pressed a hand against a tree to steady myself. It didn't help. I fell to my knees. Knives dug into my skin. All over my body. No, that was the fur forcing its way out.

Why had I agreed to this torture?

A pain worse than all the others enveloped me. It was inde-scribably horrifying.

Everything turned black.

Chapter Sixteen

Carter

I CLENCHED MY FISTS, HATING THAT I COULD DO NOTHING TO help Katya. Once she had quieted, I turned around. Hopefully she was in jaguar form.

She was. And she wasn't moving.

I raced over to her and rested my hand on her jaguar stomach. It moved up and down. She was breathing. Her body just needed to recover.

First shifts were like that.

"It's going to be okay." I kissed the top of her head, between her ears before shifting myself.

Once I was in jaguar form, Katya had lifted her head and was looking around.

I'm alive.

I nodded. *Of course you are.*

You can hear me? She rose to all fours.

We communicate through our thoughts in this form.

Is there anything else you haven't told me yet?

Probably. I can't think of everything. Come on, let's run.

She lowered her front half and stretched. *I'll follow you. You know the woods.*

Let me know if I need to slow down.

I stretched my massive paws out, then burst into a run. Katya was at my side in a matter of moments. Apparently I hadn't needed to worry about her speed.

The farther we ran, the more I felt her relax. It was taking her no time at all to settle into her new form. We raced and played, even tackling each other and rolling around in a field of wild-flowers.

It was the most fun I'd had in a long time—in any form.

After a while, we both rested on our sides. Dirt and pebbles clung to her fur, and mine as well, I assumed. We just enjoyed being in each other's presence for a while.

Then she rose and stretched, yawning.

I leaped to all fours. *Want to meet some other supernaturals?*

Can we talk to them like this too?

We'll shift back first.

Sure.

I crouched low and then burst into a run. She caught up almost immediately. We headed for the Faeble. I slowed my pace and went around to the cubbies.

She turned to me. *What are we doing?*

This is where the supernaturals are.

We're going to shift back first?

Yeah, they don't allow animals inside. That includes shifters.

What about our clothes? You promised me—

You can borrow one of the werewolves' outfits. It's fine. Are you ready to turn back?

She yawned. *I think so.*

Let me shift first, so I can grab the right clothes. I can only have you borrow from my pack.

Katya yawned again and curled up into a ball, facing away from me.

I quickly shifted back, threw on a set of my clothes, then found one of Stella's dresses. She and Katya were about the same height. Then I set it next to her.

Her bones popped and her fur retracted, showing human skin. I spun around as fast as I could, careful to keep my gaze averted so I could keep my promise of giving her full privacy.

"Are you okay over there?"

"Just trying to get used to all this. It's not as scary as I expected, actually."

"Glad to hear it." I walked over to a stack of chopped wood and studied it as though it was the most interesting thing in the history of the world. It was difficult. I was all too aware of the sounds of Katya moving around, getting dressed.

"All done."

I breathed a sigh of relief before spinning back around. Katya stood, wearing the dress. Her hair was sticking out in various directions and she had no makeup on.

She took my breath away. Her natural beauty was even more intoxicating than her perfectly-done self.

"Is something wrong?" She glanced down at herself.

"Not at all." I strode toward her, drinking in her loveliness. She held my gaze, her mouth gaping slightly. I wrapped an arm around her and threaded my fingers through her hair before closing my eyes and kissing her, taking it deeper immediately.

Katya pressed her hands on my sides and squeezed her fingers against my shirt, tickling me slightly. She kissed me back with equal passion.

I guided her to the wall and sandwiched her between it and myself. Our tongues danced together, both exploring with passion.

The door next to us snapped open, slamming against something next to it.

Katya and I jumped apart. A mesmer waggled his tongue. "Don't stop on my account."

I glared at him, then pulled Katya inside.

"What was he?" she asked. "Some kind of deranged smurf?"

"No. But their skin does kind of have a blueish hue, though."

"He's creepy."

"I couldn't agree more. Forget about him. Let's go meet Tap and Quinn."

We walked to the main part of the bar, and Katya looked around wide-eyed. I was used to the variety of the patronage, but she reminded me of a kid seeing a carnival of wonders for the first time.

"What are all these... creatures?"

"Tongue Waggler was a mesmer, basically a trickster. You're right to be wary of him. Over there at that table are mermaids and—"

"Mermaids are *real?*"

"Not so loud. Yeah, they are. They can be pretty mean, so be careful."

She stared at them. "Do they really turn into half-fish if they go into the water?"

"Yeah. Come on, let's stay focused. An entire family group of jaguar shifters are after you."

Katya turned to me, her face paling. "I almost forgot. After shifting and... Well, show me to Tad."

"Tap."

"What's he?"

"A former troll king."

"Trolls are real, too?"

I nodded. "For now, just assume every fairytale creature actually exists. Most do."

She glanced around the bar, her expression melting back to wonder. I led her to the bar and held out a stool for her to sit on.

"Tap, old buddy. I have someone for you to meet."

He spun around, carrying a tray of bubbling multi-color drinks. "Oh, yeah? Who?"

I introduced them. "Katya just found out she's a jaguar shifter. Her family of origin is in town to claim her as their own."

Concern filled his expression. "Let me give these to the mermaids, then we'll talk." He disappeared with the drinks.

Katya leaned against the counter. "He doesn't seem so bad."

"He's a good guy. He's helped my pack more times than I can count."

"If he's a king, why run a bar?"

"Former king, and he loves it. My guess is because he stays on top of what's going on with so many people coming through. Plus, he has so many people coming to him for help—I think in a way, he's still a king in his own right."

"Why'd he give up the actual position?"

"Someday, you'll have to ask him yourself."

Quinn came over and held out his hand to Katya. "I'm Quinn. Who're you?"

"Katya."

"Very nice to meet you." He turned to me. "She's the one you've been looking for?"

"Yeah. Thanks for pointing that out."

Katya laughed. "I'm glad you did, otherwise those guys might've succeeded in taking me."

Quinn's expression turned serious, and he nodded.

Tap returned and waved Katya and me over to an empty booth in the corner. Then he told Quinn to bring us some drinks.

We made ourselves comfortable, and between Katya and me we filled him in on everything.

Tap drew in a deep breath and sipped his dark-blue drink. "I heard rumors of a shifter pack in town, but hadn't actually heard any details. Do you need me to find a place to hide the lady?"

Katya scooted closer to me.

I squeezed her hand. "No, I'm going to stay with her, whether it be at the hotel or the mansion. We might need your help in other ways."

He nodded knowingly. "If the jaguars show up here, I'll let you know. Do the witches know what's going on?"

"Toby's working on that."

"Good. There's nothing like having Gessilyn on your side." He paused, looking deep in thought. "Still haven't heard from Soleil?"

I shook my head, a wave of sadness running through me at the thought of my valkyrie friend. We hadn't seen her since she risked everything using a sword that alerted her superiors in Valhalla of her location. "Do you think they found her?"

Tap frowned. "I hope not—unless she managed to find that dictator she was supposed to kill."

"That's what worries me. She wasn't even looking."

"I know." Tap turned his attention back to Katya. "She'd have been helpful, but we have plenty of other resources to keep you safe."

Katya scooted closer to me, and I wrapped my arm around her.

"But will they ever give up looking for me? Carter says they think the guy who wants to marry me thinks he *owns* me. I can hide, but that'll only slow them down, right?"

"Correct." Tap finished his drink. "Your family did a good job of keeping you hidden, but it's hard once you reach the age of shifting."

"But now that I've shifted, it'll be easier? Didn't someone say it was harder to cover my scent because I hadn't turned yet?"

Tap nodded. "That'll help, but there are ways. If they know a witch, he or she likely can work around protection spells."

"So, then what can we do now that they're here, ready to force me into a life I don't want?"

Tap and I exchanged a worried glance.

"What?" Katya demanded.

I cleared my throat. "It's going to involve a lot of death. We're going to have to kill enough of their family that the remaining ones flee. That's the only way."

Chapter Seventeen

Katya

I SHOOK, STARING AT CARTER AND TAP. "WE... WE HAVE TO *kill* them?"

"It's the jaguar way." He downed the rest of his drink.

My mind raced. "What if I just tell them I don't want anything to do with them or their lifestyle? I didn't grow up with it, and I don't want it."

Tap gave me a sympathetic glance. "You'd have about as much luck telling a dictator you don't want to follow his rules. It won't fly. They've been following their ways for many centuries. They take pride in the old traditions and will even kill their own children for breaking them."

I jumped, but it made sense. They'd murdered my dad.

"I'm sure all of this is a shock," Tap continued. "Growing up as a human with your actual human family has sheltered you from a lot. The supernatural world can be quite violent and gruesome."

I looked Carter in the eyes. "Why did you bring me into all of this?"

"He didn't," Tap said. "You were born into it. There's no getting around that. You can run, but you can't hide forever."

My stomach twisted in knots. "You're right. Sorry, Carter. I'm just so overwhelmed with all of this. I wish I could go back to not knowing."

"You think you could've avoided shifting forever? I'm surprised you made it this long."

I turned away from Tap and ran my fingertip up the glass, making a line through the condensation. "So, basically, my only choices are to fight or go with those jerks?"

"You don't have to fight," Carter said. "I can round up enough people to help us."

Indignation burned in my gut. "I'm definitely fighting. It's me they want. I'm not going to hide while others put their necks on the line for me."

Tap bore his gaze into mine. "You'll have to learn to fight. It'll take time to train."

"My final exams are coming up. I have all summer."

Carter raked his fingers through his hair and pulled. "They're already in town. I don't think we can wait that long."

Tap spun his empty glass. "It might work."

"How?" I demanded.

"We're personal friends with the high witch. She could put together a really strong cloaking spell. It would buy you enough time to finish your school year and then train. But you're going to have to focus on that alone. There won't be time for fun college activities."

"Whatever it takes to get these people, uh, jaguars out of my life. I don't want to kill anyone, but if the only other choice I have is to be someone's baby factory, then that's what they have coming."

Carter stared at me with admiration. "I don't know that I would be so brave in your situation—just finding out about the supernatural world."

"It's not like I have much of a choice. No way am I going to be some tyrant's wife. *I* control my destiny."

Tap and Carter exchanged a glance.

I gulped down the rest of my drink. "So, where do we go from here? What do I do?"

"I've got spare rooms," Tap said. "Nobody's going to find you here. You wouldn't believe the magic I have protecting my home."

"This bar is your home?" I asked.

"Downstairs. Do you want a guest room?"

I shook my head, more indignation churning. "I'm not going to let them chase me away from my home. I'm going to the hotel."

"You might want to consider it."

"I'll keep your offer in the back of my mind, but I want to live my life, not live in fear. I've got both Carter and Che there."

"But if twenty shifters show up, the two of them will be woefully outnumbered. You're not just putting your own safety on the line, but theirs. Not to mention your human family."

I hadn't thought of that. "Well, I don't want to hide. What kind of a message is *that* sending those bullies?"

Tap glanced at Carter. "How do you feel about going to the hotel with her?"

"It's what she wants. I'll bring along some of the pack members. Maybe see if Gessilyn can spare one of her siblings."

"You're both hard-headed." Tap rose. "Let me grab a concoction from downstairs. It won't last long, but it should buy you some time until Gessilyn's coven can devise a stronger protection spell."

He walked away, muttering to himself.

I turned to Carter. "You don't think I'm making a mistake, do you?"

"Standing your ground is never a mistake. I respect you for it."

A warmth ran through me. "Thank you."

Quinn came over and took our empty glasses. "Anything else I can get you?"

Carter leaned back against the booth. "I don't suppose you

have a potion to make a shifter remain permanently in his animal form?"

Quinn arched a brow. "You got some sudden desire to live out your life as a jaguar?"

"It's not for me."

Quinn snickered. "Well, I don't have anything like that, but I'll keep an ear out."

Glass shattered in another room.

"Ugh." Quinn groaned. "I better see what those mesmers are doing now."

I ran my hands over a condensation ring on the table. "Do you think we'll be able to get rid of my father's family?"

He looked deep in thought. "I'm sure of it."

"How can you be certain?"

"I've seen a lot in my time. I'm not saying this will be easy or that there won't be casualties, but it's definitely doable."

Tap returned, carrying a tear-shaped bottle with a lavender-colored liquid inside.

"What's that?" Carter asked.

"This'll keep the lady hidden from the shifters."

I eyed the bottle. "But what about Carter and Che? Will it hide me from them?"

"Only if they mean you harm."

My eyes widened. "What?"

"This will make it so your enemies can't recognize you. It won't hide you like the other spell did—the one Che has been using on you. You can talk to them, but they'll think you're someone else entirely."

"Hand it over."

"Wait," Carter said. "What do you want for it?"

Tap stared at him. "You'll owe me. One day I'll need you to drop everything and help me."

"Not until we fix this problem, right?"

"Of course."

Carter took the bottle and handed it to me. "Deal."

I watched as bubbles slowly rose. "So, I just drink this?"

"Correct. Don't leave a drop."

"How long will this last?"

"Should be the right amount to get you a week. You can get through your exams. By then, Gessilyn should have something more potent while you train."

I held the bottle up to the light. "Anything else I should know about it? Will it turn my skin blue or something?"

"No, nothing like that. You might not sleep much, however. Or maybe you will. It's hard to say how any one person will react to these things."

"More time for studying." I pulled the cork out and gulped down the lukewarm, fizzy liquid. It tasted like starfruit. Once I was done, I set it on the table.

"I was serious about not leaving a drop." Tap nodded toward the bottle, which had two tiny droplets weaving their way down to the bottom on the inside of the glass.

"Fine." I held the bottle upside down over my mouth and waited. And waited until finally I felt one drop. Then the second one. "Is that everything?"

Tap took the bottle and studied it. "Looks good." Then he turned to Carter. "You owe me. Don't forget."

"Never could."

My stomach gurgled. I belched really loudly. People turned and stared. My face burned and I covered my mouth.

"That might happen for the next hour or so," Tap said.

"I could've used a heads-up about that." I'd have done anything to keep from burping in front of Carter.

"You'll thank me later." Tap walked away and stopped at the table of mermaids.

"I'm so sorry." I couldn't look Carter in the eyes. "I'm not normally so rude."

"Don't apologize. That was impressive."

I stared at him. "Are you joking?"

He grinned. "Not in the slightest. You ready to head home?"

Energy buzzed around in me. "Yeah. Can we shift again?"

"We'd probably be better off waiting. You need to ease into it."

"So, we have to walk through the woods back to your car?" After all the running we did as jaguars, it felt like we were halfway across the globe.

"We're actually not all that far from my place."

I glanced down at the dress. "What about this? Won't your friend be mad I'm wearing her clothes?"

"She won't mind. We never put our favorites in the cubbies because other shifters caught in a bind will often borrow them."

"Like I just did."

"You can change into your clothes when we get back if you want."

"Sure, after we shift."

He laughed. "Nice try."

I shrugged. "I had to give it a shot."

Chapter Eighteen

Carter

WHEN WE ARRIVED BACK AT THE MANSION, I INTRODUCED Katya to those who were downstairs, then I gathered some things since I'd be staying at the hotel longer.

"Want anyone to go with you?" Toby asked when I got back downstairs.

"Actually, that would be great."

He nodded. "Katya filled me in. How about Sal and Jet?"

I stared at him. Sal was practically Toby's personal bodyguard and Jet was the assistant alpha. "Are you sure?"

"Sounds like you need the best."

"But what about Zia and the kids?" I asked. Jet had a family to think about.

"They're visiting the castle," Toby said. "They won't even miss him."

"Thanks," Jet quipped. "I'll have you know my family already misses me. Immensely." He headed upstairs.

"A castle?" Katya whispered.

"I'll tell you about it later."

Sal turned to Toby. "Sir, are you sure?"

"Yeah, go. Gessilyn's already working on some spells for us. You can return when she's done."

Sal gave a quick nod and headed upstairs.

Toby turned to Katya. "This is all pretty weird, isn't it?"

"You have no idea, Professor Foley."

He gave her a friendly smile. "You're in my home. Toby, please."

Katya stared at him like he'd asked her to chop off his hand.

Toby panned his palm around the living room. "Make yourself comfortable. I need to head up to my room and check on Victoria and the kids. Lakelynn's been colicky."

Katya nodded, then turned to me after Toby went upstairs. "It's so weird talking to one of my teachers so informally."

"He's a good guy. And on the bright side, if you need an extension on your math final, he'll understand."

"That's true."

Twenty minutes later, we were on the road with Sal and Jet following us in Jet's car.

Katya burped. "I'm so sorry. I tried to keep that one quiet."

I laughed. "You're adorable."

She turned away. "Stop."

"You are. I've never met anyone as charming as you. Even your blushing habit couldn't be more adorable."

Katya didn't say anything. That made my heart swell for her all the more. I'd thought I'd been in love before, but it paled in comparison to what Katya did to me.

Once we got to the hotel, I made sure Sal and Jet were settled into their room, which was as close to Katya's as possible.

Che cornered us, wanting to know what was going on. We filled him in on everything and an expression of relief covered his face. He leaned against the wall, his shoulders drooping. "You're sure that stuff will hide her?"

"Tap said it would hide her from enemies."

"I'm sure he knows what he's talking about. I'm not going to relax, though. Not until those jaguars are long gone."

"Neither am I." I stood taller. "I'm going to stay at her side until she gets sick of me and demands I leave her alone."

The corners of her mouth twitched. "I can't see that happening."

"Glad to hear it. And with all this excitement, don't forget about lunch tomorrow. Your mom really wants to celebrate your big win."

"I forgot all about volleyball." Katya shook her head. "That should be the biggest night of my life, but it was totally overshadowed by shifting."

"Shifting?" Alley appeared around the corner. She wore a dark green robe and had a black face mask covering her exposed skin.

My insides twisted in knots.

"Shifting?" Katya said. "What's that? No, I said *shopping*. Carter took me out to celebrate. Wait until you see the new clothes I got."

"Oh, show me!" Alley squealed, cracking part of her mask.

"Tomorrow." Katya yawned. "I'm exhausted."

Alley frowned. "Fine." She turned to me. "What are you, like the perfect boyfriend or something? Taking her shopping? I want to clone you so I can have some of that for myself."

My mouth dropped.

"Alley!" Katya grabbed my arm and dragged me away. Once we made it to her door, she let us in. "Can you believe her?"

"She's not so bad."

Katya plopped on the bed and patted the spot next to her. I sat and put my arm around her. She turned and pressed her mouth on mine.

I ran my hands through her hair and took possession of her mouth, needing more of her. To taste her. To experience her. I couldn't get enough. Couldn't be close enough. As our tongues danced, it felt as though we melted into one.

I'd searched so long for her, and now that I'd found her, each day it became more apparent why I hadn't been able to stop searching. We were meant for each other. I needed her just as much as she needed me, though neither of us had realized it until now.

Her hands traced their way down to my waist and she drew nearer, practically sitting on my lap. She kissed me with more passion, both fulfilling my need for more of her and making me crave more at the same time.

Katya's fingers slid underneath my shirt. She yanked it up to my chest.

I pulled back, hating myself for stopping the kiss, and fixed my shirt.

"What's wrong?" she asked.

"Are you sure you want to take this further?"

She held my gaze, then lowered it to my torso. "I couldn't be more sure."

What if it was the potion talking? If that were the case, I'd be no better than a guy taking advantage of a drunk girl. "Maybe we should slow down. At least for tonight. Your emotions are high—you won that game, your shifter family came after you, you turned for the first time. You were right when you said this was probably the biggest night of your life."

"And now I have you here in my room, all to myself. Make this best night of my life complete by giving yourself to me."

That definitely didn't sound like her. "We really should slow down. Do you want to cuddle?"

She scowled. "Do you realize what I'm offering you? And you want to snuggle?"

I drew in a deep breath. "You'll thank me later. Trust me."

Katya shook her head. "What's wrong with me? Am I just fated to be the twin nobody wants?"

"What?"

"Never mind." She jumped up from the bed, pink covering her cheeks. "I have to pee, anyway."

"Katya, I want you. More than you know. I just refuse to take advantage of you."

"Advantage of me? I'm asking for this." She stormed into the bathroom and slammed the door. Then she belched. "I'm not sorry for that one!"

She really was adorable. Even drunk on whatever magic Tap had given her.

I closed my eyes and leaned back on the pillows, kicking my feet up. Katya banged a bunch of things around the bathroom. If she'd thought it had been easy for me to pull away from her, she had never been more wrong about anything.

As I waited for her to return, my mind wandered and I drifted into a light sleep.

Lips pressing on my mouth woke me. My eyes flew open as Katya once again pulled my shirt up to my chest. Her touch tickled as it moved up.

"I'm not taking no for an answer." She nibbled my ear. "I know you want this as much as I do. You're just trying to be a gentleman. Problem is, I don't want one."

I swallowed as she tried to force my arms up to remove the shirt. She certainly made it hard to say no. "You're right about one thing. I do want this, but not now. Not like this. You're under the influence of powerful magic."

"I'm not drunk. Actually, I'm more aware than I've ever been." She whipped the shirt right over my head.

I scrambled to sit up, grabbed the shirt, and put it back on.

Katya pouted. "Don't tell me that you're a prude. Not with a body like that."

"Why don't we go look for that hidden wing?"

"*Now* you want to find it?"

"It's probably the best time to look. This late, most people will be sleeping."

She frowned. "You do have a point. Nobody's likely to find us and send us away."

"It sounds like you have experience with that."

Katya nodded. "There has to be a really good reason why an entire wing has been sealed and hidden. I intend to find out what it is."

"Then come on. Let's put your energy to good use."

She sighed. "Oh, all right."

We walked toward the 'employees only' area in silence, and she wouldn't let me put my arm around her or hold her hand.

Once we passed the rope, I looked down the hallway to the right and to the left. "Which way?"

Katya nodded toward the left. "I've been going this way lately. Not that I've made it far."

We passed the spot where the two jaguar shifters had attacked her. She stopped there and shuddered. I put my arms around her, and she let me. We stood in silence for a few moments.

Katya looked up at me. The look in her eyes told me she wanted to say something important.

"What is it?" I traced her jawline with my thumb.

"I'm sorry about the way I was acting back there. I don't know what came over me. Don't get me wrong, I'm attracted to you. I really am, but I was acting like... like... I don't know, but that was really out of character for me."

I kissed her forehead. "I'm sure it's all because of the potion. Tap tends to leave out possible side effects when he hands out those things."

She smiled sweetly. "At least I've stopped burping."

I cupped her chin. "As I said, adorable. And I'd never hold anything against you that you did under the influence of one of Tap's potions."

"I appreciate that."

"Let's get away from here. Where do you want to look for that entrance?"

Katya glanced down farther. "I've gone all the way down this portion of the hall, but not down any of the side halls yet—and there are a lot. That's the thing, this place just seems to go on forever. It's crazy to think there'd be a whole other wing."

"Why don't you guys rent out any of these rooms?"

"None of it's up to code. Mom could barely afford to update what she did. She keeps saying maybe one day."

"Maybe there's a hidden treasure in the secret wing. Then you guys could fix up the whole place."

Her eyes lit up. "Do you really think so?"

I shrugged. "Let's see what we can find."

Chapter Nineteen

Katya

WE TURNED DOWN A HALLWAY I'D NEVER EXPLORED, AND Carter stayed close to me. It looked like all the others in the non-updated sections—creepy, like something you'd see in a scary movie. I secretly expected a scary clown or a guy with a bloody knife to jump out at any point.

It was a hundred times less freaky with Carter there. Or maybe it was the fact that I could now turn into a powerful jaguar if I wanted to. A thrill ran through me at the thought.

But then again, the people who wanted to kidnap me could also turn into jaguars, and they had so much more experience at it than me. I'd only just found out that I could even do that.

"Are you okay?" Carter asked. "You're not still embarrassed about earlier?"

"Now that you bring it up..."

He chuckled. "Sorry. What are you thinking about?"

I sighed. "Everything. It's all so overwhelming."

Carter put his arm around me and kissed my cheek. "It's been a huge night. I'm sure overwhelming doesn't begin to describe it, but I'm here. Want to talk? I'll listen. Want to vent? Again, I'll listen. Or we can just explore in silence while you let everything settle."

"Are you perfect?" My cheeks warmed. Why had I said that out loud?

"I like to think so."

I burst out laughing.

We stopped walking and he looked around at the dilapidated hallway. Several of the doors had at least one number loose or missing and the walls were stained with dust, cobwebs, and who-knew-what-else. "What do you usually do when you're searching for a secret entrance?"

"It depends. Usually, I tap the walls and listen for a spot that sounds different, maybe hollow or maybe thicker. I feel around the molding for anything unusual. You never know where there might be a hidden button or something. I also like to check the rooms. Once, I found a hidden room behind a fake fireplace."

His eyes widened. "Really? What was in it?"

"Storage. Just old clothes. They weren't even that nice. It was rather disappointing. But it did give me hope that I could find more hidden areas if I kept looking. Especially with all the rumors about the hidden wing." Chills ran down my back at the thought of it.

"And you've never checked this area?"

I shook my head no.

His expression brightened. "Well, seeing that it's your lucky day, I have a good feeling about this." Carter pressed his palm on the nearest wall. "Let's do this."

We tapped walls and checked the molding all up and down the hallway.

Nothing.

He turned to me with more optimism in his expression than I felt. "Do we go down another hall, or start going through the rooms?"

"I doubt the entrance to another wing would be inside a room. Each wing starts in a hallway."

"Then let's go down another one."

Part of me wanted to give up, but it was a lot more fun to search with Carter, not to mention faster. "Okay. One more wing, then we should call it a night."

"Finally getting tired?" he teased.

I tried to hold back a grin. "Maybe."

"Good. I was getting worried that you wouldn't sleep at all for the next week."

"That wouldn't be so bad, given how much time I'm going to need to study."

We turned down another hallway. It looked exactly like the one we'd just checked.

"You sure you want to keep going?" I asked.

"This is fun." He looked like he meant it.

"Okay. Then I wouldn't mind taking you up on that snuggling offer."

"That sounds fun, too." He tapped his finger on the wall.

I went to the other side of the hallway and checked everything along the way. Again, there wasn't anything out of the ordinary. "You ready to head back?"

He turned to me. "I think I found something."

My stomach dropped to the ground. "What?"

"Yeah. Listen to this." He pressed his ear to the wall near some peeling wallpaper and tapped.

I rushed over and did the same. There was a slight echo.

We stared at each other wide-eyed.

"Your lucky night?"

"Maybe." I tapped again. There was definitely an echo.

At once, we both moved to check the molding. Carter checked the molding up at the top, near the ceiling and I checked the one near the floor.

His phone rang.

"Ignore it." My finger ran over a barely-noticeable bump on the molding.

"It's Che."

"I think I found a button!"

Our gazes locked.

"Let me just see what he needs. He wouldn't call at this hour if it wasn't important."

"That's true."

"Che," Carter answered. "What's going on? I have you on speaker."

"I need you to come down to the lobby right away." His voice sounded off. Edgy. Shaky. Completely unlike him.

"What's happening?" Carter demanded.

"Ow. Just hurry."

The call ended.

Carter held my gaze. "We'd better go."

I nodded, but snapped a couple pictures of the hallway so I wouldn't forget where we'd found the hollow spot with the hidden button. Given that I was hopped up on some magical concoction, I wasn't taking any chances.

We hurried through the maze of nearly identical creepy hall-ways until we came to the main part of the hotel and finally, down to the lobby.

Four men had guns on Che.

I cried out. Carter put an arm around me, and we rushed over.

"Put those down," Carter ordered. "Don't make me call the cops."

"You think cops stand a chance against a bunch of shifters?" He turned the gun toward Carter and me. "Where's Katya?"

I froze. They wanted me now?

So much for my lucky night.

Carter stood taller and did something with his phone behind his back. "You can't have her. She wants to stay here."

The guy laughed cruelly. "You think we care about that? She's part of *our* family. That woman is going to be my daughter-in-law and give me lots of grandsons to carry on my name."

I swallowed, trying not to shake. How dare they act as if they owned me? Anger tore through me. Even if they did manage to get me, I'd find a way to escape. No way would I live the life they had planned for me.

It was out of the question.

Footsteps sounded behind us. Jet and Sal, the two werewolves Toby had sent over, stepped beside me.

"It's time to leave." Sal's voice sounded like a growl.

"Sure. Hand over Katya."

My heart jumped into my throat.

Carter got in his face. "You can't have her. Ever. Get the idea out of your head and go back home."

"Where is she?"

Carter tilted his head. "What?"

The man stepped past him and glared at me. "You. Where is she?"

My mouth gaped. No words would come.

"You're all useless." He turned to Jet. "Where is she?"

Carter mouthed, "The potion. They don't recognize you."

Relief washed through me as I realized that was what was happening.

"Why don't you tell me?" Jet countered. "Where is Katya?"

The man scowled. "She can't be far. This is her father's hotel. He gifted it to her mother in his will. The stupid idiot mated with a human. A human!"

Anger tore through me. How dare he talk about my parents like that. I stepped up to him. "Why do you want Katya, then? She's just a stupid idiot half-human, right?"

"Stop." Carter begged me with his eyes.

I turned my attention back to the man. What was he going to do to me? He didn't even recognize me. "Isn't Katya tainted or something? Half-human and raised by humans. What an idiot."

"You're the idiot, girl! There's no half-human. Katya got the jaguar gene from Kevin. Her sister is just human. One jaguar, one human. Simple math. Move aside."

I stood my ground. "Katya doesn't want anything to do with you people. She likes the enlightened way of life the world offers her. Not your backward, woman-hating ways."

His brows came together and he struck me across the face so hard I flew backward several feet and stumbled against a wall.

In a blur, Carter attacked him, throwing him to the ground. The others all piled on top. Before my eyes, clothes flew off all the men as they turned into jaguars and werewolves.

Growls and howls echoed around the lobby. Teeth dug into fur. Blood sprayed out onto the walls and floor. Furniture knocked over.

After my shock faded, I pulled off my clothes and tried to shift. Nothing happened. I was just standing in the hotel lobby with no clothes on.

My face flamed for the twentieth time that day. I ducked behind a potted tree and closed my eyes, focusing on my jaguar self. I thought of Carter fighting for me. Bones popped, muscles burned, and finally fur sliced through my skin. I cried out and when I opened my eyes, everything was bright and all my senses were heightened.

I growled and joined the fighting. It was easy to tell the other jaguars from Che and Carter. They had a completely different scent. It was actually nearly the same as mine.

They really were my family—but only by genetics.

I leaped on top of one of them and dug my teeth into his back. The jaguar yelped and howled, but then threw me off. I skidded into the plant that had offered me privacy, knocking it over and shattering the pot.

One of the opposing jaguars stood tall and roared. Somehow, I had the sense he was calling an end to the chaos.

The other jaguars formed into human and redressed.

I ran back over to my clothes and picked them up with my

mouth. Then I headed over to the counter to turn back and get dressed out of view of the others.

While I got dressed, Che and Carter argued with the others about me.

"We're not giving up until she's in our possession."

Like I was a piece of meat. Fury churned in my stomach as I slid on my clothes.

Ding-dong.

The front door slammed shut. I rose and walked over to the guys, who were all back to human form and fully dressed.

A breeze rustled my top and chilled my skin. I looked down to find my shirt torn from sternum to bellybutton, exposing half my bra and my stomach. Apparently my jaguar teeth were sharper than I'd thought.

Embarrassed, I covered up with my arms.

"They're not going to give up." Che scowled.

"At least they can't recognize me." I tightened my arms over my top.

"For how long?" Che crossed his arms.

"A week."

"They've waited in town quietly for two weeks, maybe longer. One week isn't going to deter them."

Che turned to Carter. "Take her up to her room and make sure nobody gets close to her. I've got to clean this mess before Jennifer or any of the other staff gets down here." He swore. "And I have to do something about the security footage. We can't have anyone seeing *that.*"

"I'll help." I stood taller.

He stared at my midsection. "How? If you move your arms, your dress will expose you to everyone."

My face heated. "I can change, you know."

Che shook his head. "Just get some sleep. You need it. I didn't expect Carter to bring you down here when I called him."

I glared at him. "I'm perfectly capable of doing everything you can do. Even shift and fight those jerks."

He stared me down. "Just get some rest. I said I'll take care of everything."

Sal stepped between us and looked at me. "Jet and I will help him clean this mess. It won't take long."

I looked around him and glared at Che. "I'm not helpless."

He glared back at me. "I realize that, but you have a lot to learn. You could've gotten hurt jumping in the middle of that."

"But I didn't. And if you think I'm going to sit back and let you fight for me while I do nothing, you're as chauvinistic as they are."

Che looked like I'd slapped him. Guilt stung at me because I knew he wasn't like them at all, but I spun around and stormed toward the stairs regardless.

Carter caught up with me. "Are you okay?"

"Ugh. I wish you'd stop asking that."

"I just care."

More guilt. I ignored it and rushed up to my room. He followed me inside but I went into my closet and closed the door between us.

Why did everyone think I was so helpless? I was new to all this, but not weak or stupid. There were my relatives who thought they could stake their claim on me, then there were Carter and Che who should've been on my side, but they were too busy trying to protect me, thinking I was too helpless to do anything for myself.

They were all wrong.

Chapter Twenty

Carter

I tapped the armrest as I waited for Katya to come out of her closet. She was taking so long, I couldn't help but wonder if she'd fallen asleep in there.

I wanted to ask her if she was okay, but that had annoyed her so much downstairs, I wasn't going to make that mistake again.

Pat, pat.

Someone was outside the door.

Pat, pat, pat.

Nerves on edge, I jumped up and pressed my ear to the door.

More of the same noise. It was soft, barely noticeable, but someone was there.

I closed one eye and peeked out the peephole. Nothing appeared in the rounded glass.

Yet the sounds continued.

With one quick motion, I flung open the door.

Skittering noises sounded toward the stairs. Nobody was in the hall, but at least I'd scared off whoever had been pacing near Katya's door.

"You leaving?"

I spun around. Katya stood behind me in a long purple night-shirt. It was perfectly modest, but at the same time... just wow. I let go of the door and it closed on its own.

"Are you?" she asked.

"Am I what?" I couldn't stop looking at her.

"Never mind." She spun around and climbed under the covers.

I couldn't get my feet to move.

"Are you sleeping there or something?"

"Well, no. I could take the chair."

"Or you could join me." She turned out the lamp, surrounding us in darkness.

Even though she didn't seem to want my company, I climbed under the covers and wrapped my arm around her. Katya stiffened, but then eventually relaxed and scooted closer to me. She smelled like flowers. It was intoxicating.

I pressed my face against her hair and breathed in deeply. All my stress and worries melted away with her right there. Whether she was actually mad at me or if it was the potion, I couldn't be sure, but the fact that she at least tolerated me being with her sent a warmth through me.

Her breathing deepened, and before I knew it, I was drifting off to sleep, too.

The next morning, I woke to her gazing at me. She smiled and ran the back of her fingers along my cheek.

"I should probably shave."

She shook her head. "No, I like it."

"You do?"

"Immensely." She snuggled up to me and we lay in silence until her stomach grumbled. Her cheeks turned pink as they always seemed to.

"I love that you're so feisty, yet you embarrass easier than anyone I know."

She looked away. "Stop."

"Nothing to be embarrassed about. We all have to eat. I'm pretty hungry myself. We should also check on Che and make sure he got everything done last night."

Katya groaned. "And I'd better apologize. I acted like a spoiled brat."

I kissed her forehead. "I'm sure he understands."

"And I owe you an apology, too. I should probably just say sorry to everyone I know to be safe."

"No need to with me." I pressed our palms together and laced my fingers through hers.

"You must think I'm a bear." She shook her head and buried her face against my chest. "I've been awful the whole time you've known me. I don't know what you see in me."

I slid my finger under her chin and guided her to look at me. "What I see is a wonderfully strong woman who has more on her plate than anyone could be expected to handle. And I'm more than happy to help with that load—if you'll let me."

"You really are perfect."

"No more than you."

Katya rolled her eyes at me and climbed out of bed. That nightshirt was going to be the death of me.

An hour later, we were both showered and dressed. We strolled down to the lobby, hand-in-hand.

Everything in the lobby looked as good as new. If I hadn't known better, I'd have never guessed what had taken place the night before.

Jennifer came around from the reception desk, smiling. "Oh, good. You two are ready for lunch." She stared me down. "I didn't see you come in."

Che appeared around the corner. "I did. He arrived while you were making copies in the back."

Katya's mom relaxed. "Well, it's good to see you again. I enjoyed getting to know you better last night during the game."

She turned to Katya. "Will you text your sister? I thought she'd be down here already."

"Sure, Mom." Katya pulled out her phone and slid her finger around the screen.

Jennifer chatted excitedly about having gotten reservations at a popular restaurant outside of town.

Alley bounded into the lobby and gave Katya a big hug. "I'm so proud of you, Miss MVP!"

We piled into the taxi when it arrived, and everything went by in a blur. The others gave Katya gifts at lunch. I'd have too, if I hadn't spent every moment with her since the game, but she didn't seem to mind.

As we ate, I kept looking around for the jaguars. Che did the same. But they weren't anywhere near the restaurant. There wasn't even a whiff of them in the air. I relaxed, figuring they were taking the day to lick their wounds.

After lunch, Jennifer insisted on taking the twins out for a girls' only afternoon of shopping and pampering.

I pulled Che aside. "Is that a good idea?"

"I'll tail them and make sure they stay safe. They'll have no idea I'm watching—they never do."

"All right. I've got some calls to make, anyway. I need to follow up with Tap and Gessilyn."

Che's eyes widened. "Tap and Gessilyn are working on this? As in the former troll king and the high witch?"

"Yeah. I'm also going to see who else will help us. Toby can probably convince the vampires, who hold weight with the dragons."

"Wow. Those jaguars have no idea what they're up against."

"No, they certainly don't."

"The taxis are here," Jennifer said. "I called one to take you two back to the hotel." Her gaze landed on me. "I want to thank you."

"Me?"

"Yes. Katya has been so much happier these last two weeks since you've been in her life. You're really special to her. I just want to make sure you know that." She stared me down, clearly sending an unspoken message.

I cleared my throat. "She's really special to me, too. I just want what's best for her."

Che stepped a little closer to me. "Don't worry, Jen. I've already given him 'the talk.' He's got my seal of approval."

Jennifer smiled and turned back to me. "You seem like a really great guy, but you have to understand why I'm so protective of her. The girls are all I have of my Kevin."

"I do, and I would never treat her as less than the treasure she is."

She threw her arms around me, then turned to pay the bill.

"Wait," I said. "I've got that."

Her eyes widened. "What?"

I pulled out my card and handed it to the server before turning back to Jennifer. "My treat."

"But... why?"

My mind raced. I didn't want to hurt her pride by saying that I knew she didn't have a lot of money and that I had plenty to spare. "It's my gift to Katya for the win."

"I don't know what to say. Thank you. You really do seem to be as great as Katya thinks."

"It looks like the taxis are here," Che said.

We gathered our things, and I signed the receipt as everyone headed for the door.

Once outside, Katya wrapped me in a hug. "Thank you for paying for the meal. I know it was more than Mom could afford, and she planned a spa day on top of lunch."

"She just wants you to feel as special as you are." I gave her a quick kiss.

"Come on, Katya!"

She brushed her lips across mine. "I'll be back to the hotel as soon as I can."

"Have fun." Our gazes lingered as she climbed into the taxi with her mom and sister.

Che turned to me. "You take the taxi. I'm going to hail another one and keep an eye on them."

"Sounds good. Give me a call if you need anything."

He nodded, and we waved as the ladies' taxi pulled away. "And you tell me if you hear any good news from Tap or Gessilyn. I still can't believe that. And you mentioned the dragons?"

"They're a maybe. Toby has sway with the vampire queen, who is mother-in-law to a dragon king."

"Well, I'm glad to hear that. Blown away, but glad." Che waved to a taxi.

A breeze blew by, and with it, the scent of jaguar shifters tickled my nose.

Che and I exchanged a worried glance.

I shuddered. "You keep an eye on her, and I'll find out what I can about who can help us."

He sniffed the air. "Make sure they know it's urgent."

"Believe me, I will."

Chapter Twenty-One

Katya

I SET THE PEN DOWN ON THE DESK AND TOOK A DEEP BREATH. My last final was complete. Summer vacation would start as soon as I walked out the door of the classroom.

Yet instead of freedom, doom pressed on all sides.

It had been a full week since I drank Tap's potion. I'd run into my relatives a couple times over the week, but not once did they recognize me. I wasn't sure who they thought I was, but it clearly wasn't me.

That was about to change, and I wasn't sure when. Would the potion last *exactly* one week? Down to the hour? Or in general, like it might fade, making me safe for another day?

At least now I had time to worry about it. It would be another three months before I needed to think about studying again. With any luck, by then all these troubles would be long forgotten.

Or would I be a slave wife to a dictator-like husband who wouldn't give me enough freedom to attempt an escape?

I shook my head. No, I couldn't let myself think like that. That wouldn't happen. It wasn't even in the realm of possibility.

Except it was.

"Time's up." The professor's voice broke through my thoughts. "Turn in your papers and have a nice summer."

Nice summer. Right.

I stuffed my pen into my bag and took my exam to the front desk along with everyone else, who were just as eager to get out the door.

As soon as I made it to the hallway, Carter smiled at me. I relaxed just seeing him. He'd been my constant companion all week, never leaving my side. Each night, I slept snuggled against him, and we really only parted to use the bathroom or get dressed.

He pulled a bouquet of colorful tulips from behind his back. "Congratulations! You made it through finals."

I ignored the flowers and kissed him deeply, releasing all my pent-up emotions into his minty-sweet mouth.

Someone whistled behind us. Another person shouted for us to get a room.

Carter grinned and handed me the bouquet. "They're just jealous that I get to kiss the most beautiful woman on campus."

I leaned my forehead against his and gazed into his eyes. "Or maybe they envy *me* for kissing you."

He laced his fingers through mine. "I don't see why they would."

"We'll just have to agree to disagree."

"I guess so."

"You two are so cute, I can't stand it."

I turned from Carter to see Paige standing next to us.

Her mouth dropped. "Flowers? She's right. You *are* perfect."

"Told you so." I played with Carter's hair. "So, are you going home for the summer?"

Paige shook her head. "I'm taking a summer class and am going to keep working at my internship."

"We'll have to hang out."

"For sure! We can do a double-date soon. You still haven't met Pax yet."

"No, I haven't." I made sure to use an accusatory tone.

She laughed. "Call me. I have to get to my Physics final."

"Ugh. Good luck."

"I'm gonna need it!"

We waved, then headed outside where the sun's rays beat down on us. It was almost enough to make me forget about my problems. Almost.

"When will the potion stop protecting me?"

He put a fingertip to my mouth. "You can't just say things like that with all these people around."

"Nobody's paying attention. Everyone's thinking about exams or summer break."

"Still." He pressed his lips against mine. "We have to be careful."

"Okay, okay. But seriously, when will it stop?"

"Not until tonight."

"Then what?"

"We find another way to keep you safe."

I stepped back. "You don't know what, though? What about that witch, or Tap or—?"

He pulled me close and whispered in my ear, tickling it. "We can't talk about witches in front of mere mortals, either. Stop worrying for now, and come see what I've been planning."

"What?" I stepped back and stared at him.

His eyes shone with excitement. "Promise to stop worrying?"

"Do you promise I'll be safe?"

"Yes." He spoke with such confidence that I had to believe him.

"Okay. What did you plan?"

"You'll have to wait and see." He took my hand and led me across campus to his Ferrari. Even though I'd ridden in it a handful of times, I still couldn't get used to seeing it.

Carter held the passenger door open for me and gave a slight bow. "M'lady."

I climbed inside and drew in a deep breath, taking in the strong leather scent.

"Where are we going?" I asked after he started the engine.

"You'll find out soon enough."

"When I told Paige that you're perfect, what I really meant was annoying."

He chuckled. "Whatever you have to tell yourself. I'm still not telling you where we're going until we get there."

"Like I said, annoying."

"I'll take that."

Before long, he pulled onto the dirt road heading for his home—not that he'd stayed there a single night since I'd met him.

"You're taking me to the mansion?"

He shook his head. "It's merely a parking lot as far as my plans are concerned."

"We're going into the woods?"

"You're the most curious person I've ever met, you know that?"

"I'll take that," I teased, using the same expression he had when I'd called him annoying. "Are we going to shift again?"

We'd shifted a couple times during the week when my anxiety over the final exams got to me. Each time was more exhilarating than the last.

"Nope."

"What, then?"

He shook his head, parked, then helped me out.

"Going for a hike? I'm not really dressed for that." I glanced down at my sundress and heeled sandals.

"You're fine. We're not going too far into the woods."

"Ha! So we *are* going into the woods."

Carter snickered. "You got me. Yes, we are, but that's all you're getting out of me."

He wrapped his arm around me, and we strolled into the

woods, following a well-traveled path. I continued questioning him, but he kept his lips sealed.

Then he led me down a sloping, ivy-covered path to a pond that shone in the sunlight. Several rainbows reflected from it, and a unicorn lapped up water from the other side. A unicorn.

My mouth dropped open. "Unicorns are real?"

"That surprises you?" He cupped my chin and kissed me lightly. "Look over here."

I followed his gaze to an elaborate picnic setup on top of a large purple and green blanket. A bottle of champagne leaned against the fancy basket. "You set this up?"

"I did, and I even had Emery watch it to make sure the unicorn stayed away from the food."

"Where is he?" I glanced around, not seeing the red-haired werewolf.

"I told him to take off as soon as we showed up." Carter stepped closer, pressing himself against me. He wrapped his arm around me and kissed me, our tongues dancing and exploring.

My pulse raced through my body, and I returned the kiss with equal passion. Birds sang nearby, almost in tune with our expression of love.

I froze. Was what we had actually *love*?

Carter ran his fingertips along my jawline. "Is this okay?"

"It's better than okay." I took possession of his mouth again and raked my fingers through his hair.

The word love rolled around in my mind, soaring higher and making me feel like Carter and I were floating in the air. I really did love him. Though we'd only known each other for less than four weeks, we'd hardly been apart. We were much closer than a normal couple of only a month.

Carter pulled back and stared at me, gasping for air. "Maybe we should see what's in the picnic basket."

I struggled to find my voice. "You don't know what's inside?"

He kissed my nose, and led me over to the blanket. "I do, but you don't."

We sat, and he opened the basket. Carter pulled out plates, champagne flutes, and an array of foods. The aromas made my mouth water.

"Laura made everything, so I know it's going to be delicious." He dished up lasagna, creamy vegetables, fruit kabobs, and chocolate chip cookies. Everything except the fruit released steam when he opened the containers. "I hope you're hungry."

I stared into his eyes. "Oh, I definitely am."

We leaned against each other and watched the water and the unicorn while we ate. It was like a dream, and I never wanted to wake up.

After we finished eating, Carter popped the champagne and filled the flutes. He held up his. "To us."

I tapped my flute against his. "To love."

His eyes widened.

So did mine. I hadn't meant to say love. I'd meant to say *us*. But 'love' had come out instead. And now he was staring at me with that shocked expression.

"Love?"

If I could've found my voice, I'd have said any number of things. Instead, I said nothing.

"Love?" His voice was softer this time.

I nodded and opened myself up to the probable rejection. "I love you, Carter. I know it may seem crazy after only a few weeks, but—"

He pressed his lips on mine and kissed me with such passion it sent both heat and a shiver through me. Then he gazed into my eyes. "I've loved you since the moment I laid eyes on you. *That* probably sounds crazy, but I believe we're meant to be together."

It took a few moments to register his words. He loved me too? He thought we were meant for each other?

I opened my mouth to speak, but he kissed me again, stopping me from saying anything.

Chapter Twenty-Two

Carter

I HANDED LAURA THE PICNIC BASKET. "THANK YOU. Everything was delicious, as always."

She beamed. "I'm so glad. How did the picnic itself go?"

It was my turn to beam. "She told me she loves me." It was easy to open up to our pack mom because she'd grown to feel like my actual mom.

Her entire expression glowed. "Must be the love potion I put in there."

My smile faded. "What?"

She kissed my cheek. "I'm kidding, sweetie. It's all you. What's not to love?"

I breathed a sigh of relief. "Don't do that to me, Mom."

"I can't help it. You're fun to tease."

"Can I do anything to help clean up?"

She shoved me out of the kitchen. "Just go enjoy your girl. I've got this."

Toby nearly walked into me. "Carter, I didn't realize you were here. I have to talk to you." He glanced around. "Privately."

I followed him to his office, first checking on Katya. She sat in the living room with Victoria, Ziamara, and the group of kids. They were all laughing, and she didn't even notice me.

Toby closed his office door behind us and indicated for me to have a seat on his couch. He sat two cushions away and took a deep breath.

"Is something wrong?"

"It's less than ideal, but we have options."

I groaned. "Lay it on me."

"Gessilyn got called away in the middle of working on a cloaking spell for Katya. Her family's working on something, but they don't have anything yet. They say to give them another day or two."

"What?" I exclaimed. "Why is a simple spell so difficult?"

"It's extra-complicated hiding a jaguar shifter from her own family members, apparently. The details went over my head, but they're working on it. Tap says she can stay in his guest room for as long as she needs to. Nobody will find her there."

I nodded, my mind racing. "Maybe Tap's place is the answer."

"Or I can see if the vampires will house her. They won't let a pack of enemy shifters near the castle. Plus, she might enjoy spending time there. She's probably never seen the world's largest castle."

"Tap's place is closer. I think that's our best bet. He might even have some more of the potion he gave her last week."

Toby nodded and gave me a sad smile. "She's also welcome here. So are you."

"I hope so—I live here."

"Do you? I haven't seen you in weeks."

"Yes. This is my pack, my family. I just need to stay close to Katya to make sure she stays safe."

Toby nodded knowingly. "I understand. Whatever you decide,

let me know. Also, the second I hear from Gessilyn's family, you'll be the first to know."

"I appreciate that." I clenched my fists and rose. "Have you gotten ahold of other werewolf packs? We might need the backup sooner than expected if Katya has no cloaking spells."

"You could always ask Darrell at the spice shop, though I suspect Katya has become immune to his concoctions. Otherwise, neither you nor the other jaguars would've found her."

I nodded. "Right. I'm going to talk with her about staying at the Faeble."

Katya was still playing with the kids. I sat next to her, and little Wilder climbed onto my lap.

"Where you been, Uncle Carter? I miss you."

"Aw," Katya gushed. "I'm sorry, Wilder. I've been keeping him away. We'll stay so you can play with him."

"Yay!" Wilder threw his tiny fist into the air and knocked me over flat on my back. The kid loved nothing more than wrestling.

An hour later, Katya and I headed outside. She turned to me. "I don't know about you, but I'm ready to drop from exhaustion. My bed never seemed more welcoming."

"About that..."

Her eyebrows came together. "What do you mean?"

"Tap's protection spell is going to wear off anytime now, and we don't have another one to replace it."

"What are you getting at?"

"I think we should take Tap up on his offer to stay in his guest room."

"What? No."

"It's only temporary. Gessilyn needs only a day or two to come up with a spell for you."

Katya's mouth formed a straight line, and she shook her head. "I won't go."

"Why not? Your family will find you without protection in place."

"They're not my family. Just relatives. Big difference."

I nodded, understanding completely. "Still, they're dangerous, and we're not ready to face off with them."

She dug her heel into the ground. "I am. I'll have no problem telling them where they can stick their old ideas."

"Can we sleep on it? I hear Tap's guest room is amazing."

"I don't care. I'm not letting those jerks scare me away."

Why had I thought convincing her to stay at the Faeble would be easy? I took a deep breath. "They've brought in a lot of shifters. The scent is strong, and continues to grow stronger every day."

"I've noticed, but that doesn't change my mind."

"Even though what they want is to take you away?"

"Have you noticed they haven't been successful? I'm still here."

Irritation ran through me. I took a deep breath and squeezed her hand gently. "But now they're amping up their game. It's probably going to get ugly. When I faced off against my dad, his wildly popular club burned to the ground."

She held my gaze for a moment. "The Jag?"

"How did you know?"

"I've heard about it. It was really exclusive, then one day a mysterious fire destroyed it. There are a lot of theories flying around about it."

"The truth is, it was a battle of the shifters. Jaguars and Wolves, mostly."

"Wait." Her eyes widened. "Your last name is Jag, and it was called the Jag. I never made the connection before."

"It's not a big deal. My point is that things can get ruined—lives will end. What if it's your hotel? Your family?"

Katya's eyes widened further.

"All I'm asking is that you hide out in the Faeble for a couple days until Gessilyn can work her magic. Once she does, she'll have such a powerful cloaking spell that your fam—your relatives will think you've moved somewhere else. Then, so will they."

"I understand what you're saying. How about this bargain—?"

"You want to set a wager when your safety is involved?"

"Just hear me out." She pleaded with her eyes.

I took a deep breath. "What is it?"

"Keep in mind that Tap's potion is good through tonight—"

"We hope. It's not an exact science. It probably won't end exactly at the same time you took it last week."

"But probably pretty close. I've been waiting all week to get back to that secret entrance we found. I'd have been there if I hadn't needed to study so desperately. If we go check it out, I'll hide out at Tap's after."

I frowned. "That's the only way you'll agree to stay at the Faeble?"

She crossed her arms and nodded yes.

"Okay. On the condition that if we sense more shifters, we leave immediately. Your safety first."

Katya sighed. "Oh, all right."

We climbed into my car and headed for the hotel. I kept my senses on high alert for other jaguar shifters, but we seemed to be in the clear. The potion was still protecting her—for now.

When we arrived at the hotel, the lobby was packed.

"Some convention on campus," Katya told me. "We're booked."

I sniffed the air. The only jaguar shifters were Che, Katya, and me. I relaxed a little, then we headed to the off-limits area. The halls were like a maze with so many twists and turns, and each one looking the same. Even with our keen senses, it was hard to find the exact place we'd been a week prior.

Katya pulled out her phone and found the pictures. By some miracle, we managed to find the spot by following room numbers.

We both stared at the spot, and it all came back to me. The empty-sounding wall and her finding a button on the molding. I tapped the wall and listened.

It echoed.

She looked at me with a mixture of excitement and trepidation.

"Are you ready?" I tapped another section of the wall. It was solid. Only the one spot appeared to be echoing.

"Let's do this." She knelt down and ran her fingers across the molding.

I stared at the wall, my mind and pulse both racing. What were we going to find? A horrible thought struck me. What if we unleashed a new enemy? There had to be a reason for an entire wing being sealed off.

"Help me out here," Katya said.

I knelt and felt along the molding. "You're sure about this?"

"I've been searching for as long as I've lived here. I *have* to know if there's really a secret wing that someone went to such great lengths to hide."

"You don't think it's meant to stay hidden?"

"Carter, you sound like my mom."

Maybe Jennifer was wiser than Katya gave her credit for, but I didn't bother saying anything. It was clear there was no point in trying to convince Katya this could be a bad idea. I could only hope that whatever was sealed and hidden away was harmless.

Because people always went to such great effort to hide things that were no threat. I braced myself. Hopefully, we weren't about to multiply our problems.

Katya studied her phone's screen. "The button should be right here."

My finger brushed over a slight bump in the molding. "Maybe this is it."

She frowned. "That's not where it was last week. It was right here." She pointed to a spot about a foot away.

"A lot has happened between then and now."

"Enough to make a button move?"

"Or to make us forget."

Katya shook her head. "I wouldn't forget something this important."

"Well, I found something right here." I pressed on the bump but nothing happened.

"That's because what I found before was an actual button. Not a bump." Katya pressed her palm along the molding. "Found it!"

I waited as she pushed on it.

"Nothing." She frowned and pressed harder, more rapidly. "Come *on*."

"Maybe it has something to do with what I found." I pushed on the bump and it did nothing.

We both pressed down simultaneously.

Creak.

Katya and I stared at each other, wide-eyed.

Creak. Creeeeeak.

Crack!

I jumped back, pulling Katya with me.

The wall shook and kicked off dust, but didn't move.

Katya stepped closer to me. "Is it going to open?"

Creak, creak.

I put my arm around her and prepared myself to jump in front of her at a moment's notice. "I think we're about to find out."

The wall shook again, then moved away from us like a door opening to the inside.

It revealed a dark hallway with dark green shag carpeting. A musty odor escaped.

Katya stared at me, not saying anything.

I pulled out a small flashlight attached to my keychain. "Do you want to go in?"

Chapter Twenty-Three

Katya

MY MUSCLES ALL FROZE, LEAVING ME UNABLE TO BUDGE.

"Katya?"

I couldn't even look at Carter. My body was stuck facing the now-open wall. I'd spent so long hoping to find the secret wing. Now I wasn't sure I could face it.

Maybe I should have listened to Carter and gone to Tap's. What if he was right about not wanting to find out what was inside?

Could it be worse than my shifter relatives?

"Katya?" Carter repeated. "We can always come back. Nobody else knows what we've found. We—"

"No." I sucked in a deep breath. "We've made it this far. Walking away would be foolish."

"So, you want to go in?" He tugged on my arm.

I didn't move.

"The wing isn't going anywhere. We can always grab a bite to eat and think this over."

"No. Let's do this." I took a deep breath, allowing it to reach every inch of me. Then I stepped toward the dark hallway.

Carter kept his arm around my shoulder, and we stepped into the dark, musty hall together. The blackness clung to us like a heavy weight, pressing on all sides.

"It reeks of illness," Carter whispered.

"Sickness has a smell?"

"Yeah. It's that pungent odor in the air."

I sniffed the air and sucked in dust. After coughing, I sneezed twice. "Well, I guess if anyone's living here, we've alerted them that they have company."

He squeezed my shoulder. "If they're as ill as they smell, I doubt they can do much damage. Though I have to wonder how anyone could survive in here for so long, especially when sick."

"They could infect us. Or what if it's the ghost? The one that tried to drown me?"

"Do you want to turn back?" he asked.

"No way. Anyway, I'm fully vaccinated."

"There might be a disease from a long time ago. Something nobody can protect us from."

"I know you can't see me, but I'm glaring at you."

"I'm just saying it could be anything." He turned on his flashlight. It shone a small beam, exposing very little. More doors, just like all the others.

Though it should've felt familiar, a chill ran down my spine, and I shivered. It may have looked the same, but it wasn't at all.

We crept down the hallway, only able to see what Carter's tiny flashlight exposed.

"Is there a way to turn on the lights in here?" He stopped.

I nearly bumped into him. "I wouldn't know. It's my first time here, too."

"How do you turn on the lights in the other sections?" He shone the beam slowly up and down the wall. "I don't see any light switches."

I thought for a moment. "There's a master set of lights in the employee's area of the lobby."

"And there's nothing for a wing that nobody knows about? I'd think that'd answer everyone's questions about this wing."

"So would this." I panned my hands around us. "I don't know anything about that control panel. It might just be a general set that turns it on for the whole building."

"But you'd think there'd be something separate for each wing."

"Don't ask me. I'm not some electrical wizard. Plus, I can't explain how people from a hundred years ago or more thought about wiring this huge building."

"True." He started walking again. "If the lights are connected, I'm sure they burned out years ago. Let's see what we can find."

The farther we crept, the closer I moved to Carter. Goose bumps had formed on my arms, and they weren't going away.

It seemed to take forever because he shone the little light everywhere. Had the wing not been sealed off and dark, it'd have been just like all the others.

We both froze simultaneously.

A light moan sounded. Where from, was the question.

I held my breath, waiting. Listening.

It sounded again. I couldn't tell where it came from.

A million questions ran through my mind, but not one found its way to my mouth.

Part of me wanted to run. The rest of me wanted to find out who or what was moaning in a place that had been sealed off for decades, maybe longer. My feet didn't move.

Moan.

I grabbed onto Carter's arm. He put a finger to his mouth and glanced around.

One long moan sounded. We both pointed to a door on our left.

My mouth went dry, and my tongue stuck to the roof of my mouth.

Carter walked toward the door, nearly dragging me since I couldn't get my body to cooperate.

I'd been the one insistent on finding the answers. Now I was nothing more than a scaredy-cat. I could shift into a jaguar but now feared the dark.

Carter reached for the doorknob. I held my breath, my mouth somehow managing to grow drier.

He shone the light up and down the door. There was nothing special about it. He grasped the knob.

I clung to his arm, but at the same time, I was prepared to run. Run, and never look back. Although if we'd just woken some ancient evil, running probably wouldn't do me any good.

A chill ran down my spine. The temperature seemed to drop ten degrees.

Carter twisted the doorknob.

It actually turned.

I stared in horror.

Why had I been so insistent? So curious? If I'd have stopped for a moment to think about it, I'd have remembered that curiosity killed the cat.

Carter and I were both part jaguar. Members of the cat family.

What had I done?

There was no turning back now.

Carter pushed the door open.

The moaning grew louder.

I wanted to grab Carter and pull him down the hallway, close the hidden door, and never return. Maybe live out the rest of our days in Tap's spare room.

Instead, Carter walked into the room.

I stared at his back, unable to speak.

"Katya," he said. "You have to come see this."

"Katya?" came a dry, ragged voice. "Katya's here?"

Whatever it was, it wanted me.

Chapter Twenty-Four

Katya

"KATYA," CALLED THE RASPY VOICE.

Despite everything inside me screaming to run, I took a step toward the open door. Then another. My heart pounded against my chest, threatening to break through.

Finally, I made it inside. Carter shone a light onto a bed, where the figure of a person lay.

"Katya? Is that you?" The owner of the ragged voice didn't budge.

"Y-yes."

"Come closer."

My heart beat even faster. It was actually going to burst out of my chest. Yet I managed to creep closer to the bed.

Carter took my hand in his, and together we walked toward the bed. He kept the weak beam of light aimed at the figure.

"Is that really you, Katya?"

I didn't dare answer. Who knew what the admission would lead to?

As we neared, the faint light revealed a frail man, practically skin and bones.

"Katya?" He reached for me.

"Who are you?" Carter shone the flashlight directly on his face.

I recognized his face. I'd stared at his picture every single day of my life. As my gaze locked with his, I knew I was right.

"Who are you?" Carter repeated.

"Dad." My knees gave out, and I crumpled to the dusty ground. "Is it really you?"

"It's me, baby. Come here."

I couldn't pull myself to my feet, so I crawled toward the bed.

Carter stepped between us. "How do we know you're really her dad? Why have you been here all this time? You're supposed to be dead."

I craned my neck to see around him.

"I practically am, wouldn't you say?" Dad struggled to sit up. "I've missed my daughters' entire childhoods. That's a fate worse than death. And Jennifer, how is she? Did she live a happy life? What about Che?"

Tears welled in my eyes, blurring my vision. I sprang to my feet and leaped for the bed. Carter put out his arm to stop me, but I wouldn't let anything get in between my dad and me.

I threw my arms around his thin frame and clung to him, tears flowing like never before. "Daddy."

"My little Katya. You're not so little anymore, though."

"You've been here this whole time?"

He nodded his head. "I was trying to keep you girls and your mom hidden from my family when they found me. They locked me in this wing, making it so that I couldn't get out."

"How have you survived?" Carter asked. "Has someone been feeding you?"

"A curse was placed on me. As long as I'm in the hotel, I cannot die—no matter what happens. I've had nothing to eat or drink for, what, twenty years?"

I choked back a sob. "Almost. What if you leave the hotel? Will you live?"

He coughed. "I can live normally outside the hotel. But inside, no matter what is done to me, I will not die. That is my curse."

I gasped.

"How did you find me?" he asked.

"Mom brought us here five years ago, and we've been running the hotel. Well, not the whole thing. Just the front wing."

"You've been here for five years?" Dad's voice cracked.

"Can you walk?" Carter asked. "We need to get you food. You probably need medical care. What about shifting?"

"I haven't walked in years."

My heart shattered. I buried my face into Dad's shoulder. "I can't believe they did this to you."

Carter put his hand on my shoulder. "Those are the same people who are after you."

"I know, but I'd never do this to someone in my family. Ever!"

Dad kissed my cheek. "That's what makes us different from them, my baby."

I sprang to my feet. "I have to get Mom and Alley! They're never going to believe this."

"Bring me to them. I don't want to spend another moment in here."

"You can't even walk." I shook my head vigorously. "We'll send for food. An entire banquet. Whatever it takes to get you on your feet." I embraced him again. "Don't move."

"That won't be a problem."

I spun around and put my hand on Carter's arm. "Don't leave him, okay?"

"You can't go alone."

"My presence is hidden! He needs me, and I won't let *him* be alone. I'm trusting you, Carter. Please stay with him."

"I will."

Tears blurred my vision again as I raced out of the secret wing and made my way to the main part of the hotel. I got turned around at one point and had to double back around. It was like the hotel had been designed to confuse people.

I ran past a large mirror before the stairs down to the lobby and caught sight of my reflection. I was a complete mess, with streaks of dust on my arms and face and my hair sticking out in several directions. That was in addition to my smeared makeup and red, puffy eyes.

Downstairs, Mom and Alley were talking on either side of the reception desk in the otherwise empty lobby.

"Kat, what's wrong?" Mom exclaimed.

"Dad." I gasped for air.

They both looked at me like I'd lost my mind.

"He's here." I pointed toward the stairs.

"Dad's here?" Color drained from Alley's face.

Mom shook her head. "He's dead, Kat."

"No, he's not. He's been in the hidden wing all this time."

"Hidden wing?" Mom stared at me. "That's only a myth."

"It's not. We found it, and Dad's there. He's asking about both of you. He needs food."

"Kevin's alive?" Che asked from behind.

I spun around. "Yes! He's in the hidden wing."

"You believe her?" Mom sputtered.

Che's expression tightened. "There's a lot you don't know. For your own safety."

Alley grabbed hold of my hand. "He's really here? Alive?"

I nodded, tears stinging my eyes again. "It's really him."

"Take us to him. Where's the hidden wing?"

I ran up the stairs. Their footsteps thundered behind me.

"How is this possible?" Mom asked. "I was there when he was buried."

"We buried a body burned beyond recognition," Che said.

"It was him. Remember, they proved it with his molars? The dental records proved it without a doubt."

"The teeth were inside his mouth, but not attached to his gums, Jennifer. Think about it—they were probably planted."

Mom cried out.

We ducked under the rope and I led them through the maze of halls and doors that looked exactly the same. In the confusion, we circled around a couple times, passing through the same corridor twice. I hoped they wouldn't notice.

"Haven't we been here before?" Mom asked.

"These stupid hallways all look the same," I grumbled. "We need to paint them different colors, or do something to make it easier to tell them apart. Oh, wait. We turn here."

A few more minutes later, we turned down the hallway that led to the secret wing.

Only there was no open wall.

I stared at the spot where we should've been able to go inside.

"What?" Mom demanded.

"It should be right here." I pressed myself against the wall and tapped. It just sounded like a normal wall. No emptiness. No echoing.

I tapped harder, then pounded with all my might.

"It has to be right here. Right here!"

Mom leaned against another wall and slid to the ground. "Why are you doing this to me, Katya? Playing with my emotions like this? You know how much I loved your father. So much that I've never been able to look at another man romantically." She brought her hands to her face and sobbed.

Alley looked at me like I was some kind of monster.

"He's here! I'm not making this up." I pounded on the door, desperation building.

Che pulled me away from the door. "Katya."

I yanked my arm away from him. "Dad's here! I wouldn't lie about this. How can you guys think I would?"

Mom glanced up at me and wiped her eyes, smearing mascara across her face. "Dad's dead, Katya. Maybe you saw someone else, but he's gone."

"You're just cruel." Alley sniffled.

I glared at Che. He had to believe me. The one person who knew about the supernatural world.

His expression was filled with disappointment.

I crumpled to the ground. "Dad! Carter!"

"Don't do this." Alley helped Mom up. "After everything we've all been through, how dare you?"

"I'm telling you the truth."

Alley narrowed her eyes. They shone with tears. "This is low. You need to stop, sis. Now."

"He's in the secret wing!"

"There's no hidden wing. It doesn't exist. Just go. Leave us all alone. I don't know why you're doing this." She and Mom turned their backs on me and wandered down the hall.

"He's really here. I swear." Why didn't they believe me? It was like they were under a spell.

A spell. That had to be it.

I rose and pounded on the wall again. "Dad!"

Once they saw him, they would have to believe me.

Alley stormed over to me, grabbed my shirt and yanked me back. "Stop this now, Katya. I can't believe you'd keep up this charade."

Mom pulled her away from me. "She might not be able to help herself."

"What?" Alley stared at her.

Mom took a deep breath. "Shortly after Dad's funeral, his dad —your grandpa—came to me."

"What?" Che exclaimed. "You never told me."

"I don't have to tell you everything. You came to help me with the girls, and I appreciate it, but you're not actually part of this family."

Che looked like she'd slapped him with her words. "Are you feeling yourself, Jennifer?"

"I've been in contact with Kevin's family every so often over the years. They told me the truth, Che. The truth you never did." Her nostrils flared.

His mouth gaped. So did mine.

Mom knew about us being shifters?

"What secret is that?" Che demanded.

I took a step back, keeping my gaze on Alley who was about to learn a truly shocking secret.

Mom glared at Che, then turned to me with a sad expression. "Mental illness runs in your father's side of the family. It's from your grandmother's side, Katya. None of you can do anything about it, but you've inherited it from him."

I couldn't even blink. Mental illness? She thought we had a mental disorder?

"Your grandpa told me the signs to look for in you girls, and you have every single one, Kat. I was hoping he was wrong, but I can't keep burying my head in the sand any longer. It's time to get you the help you need."

"What?" I exclaimed. "I don't need help!"

She frowned. "Honey, you're banging on a wall, screaming for your long-dead dad. I know you girls wish you got a chance to know him—believe me, there's nothing more I want for you two. But there's nothing any of us can do."

I pulled out my phone and found the picture of the secret wing's hidden door and compared it to the wall in front of me. "Wait. This is the wrong wall. It's the wrong wall!"

Mom put her hand on my arm and squeezed. "We need to get you help before this progresses any further. Your grandpa knows a doctor who is familiar with your family's illness. He can help us get you what you need. He already gave me one thing."

I stared at her in disbelief. "What I need is to show you where the hidden wing really is!"

"Why do you believe them when you know Dad didn't trust them?"

"He had the mental illness too. It turns people against their families."

My mouth dropped. "That's crazy! Listen to yourself."

Alley stepped closer to me. "You're the one who thinks our dead dad is alive."

"He *is* alive! I'll show you."

"Stop this." Alley grabbed my other arm.

I looked to Che for help. He surely couldn't go along with this. Not when he knew how dangerous my grandfather was. In fact, my grandfather had probably done something to turn my mom against me—maybe a potion similar to the one Tap had given me.

Mom turned to him. "I need you to go downstairs to the lobby. A huge group is due right about now, and I'm in no state to greet guests."

"I really shouldn't leave right now."

"I'm your boss, and I said to go!" She glared at him.

Che nodded. "I'm going to find someone who can take care of the guests and be right back."

I stared at him in stark disbelief. How could he abandon me now?

He threw me an apologetic glance and left.

"Mom, you've got to listen to me." Anger and fear ran through me. I pulled away and bones popped.

Mom's face paled. "I've been trying to pass that popping off as normal for an athlete. That's what I wanted to believe. But according to your grandpa, it's one of the main signs of this particular illness."

"No, you don't understand. He's lying."

"I'm sorry to have to do this." She reached into her purse.

I should have run, but again my feet failed me.

My mom pulled out a syringe and stuck it into my arm. "This is for your own good, honey. Your grandpa promises it will help."

Everything went blurry. And cold.

Then black.

Chapter Twenty-Five

Carter

"SHOULD IT TAKE HER THIS LONG?" KEVIN ASKED.

It had taken twice as long as I'd have thought, but I didn't want to worry him. "Maybe she couldn't find them, or maybe they're busy with hotel guests. It could be anything."

"Or they might not believe I'm still alive. I wouldn't put it past my father to come up with something elaborate and convincing. Something that would leave nobody with any doubt that I was dead and gone."

"Still, there's no reason for them to doubt Katya. She's smart and level-headed. They all adore her."

"You should go and find her." He lay back down on the bed.

"I promised her I wouldn't leave you alone."

"I've been alone for nineteen years. What's another few minutes?"

"No. I can't risk something happening to you. Katya would never forgive me. Neither would I, actually."

"Then take me with you."

"But if she comes back, and we're not here..." My voice trailed off. There didn't seem to be a good solution. Then I thought of something. "I'll just text her. Let her know I'm moving you."

"We just can't stay here. That's all I ask. I have a bad feeling."

I couldn't deny that my inner sirens were wailing. Katya should've been back or at least tried to contact me by now.

No service.

"What's the matter?"

"I don't have a signal. This wing must be blocking it—the same magic that's kept you hidden. It's the only thing to make sense."

"Let's go, then." Kevin struggled to sit.

I offered him my arm and helped him to his feet.

"Thanks. I gave up trying years ago."

"So, you *can* walk?"

"Yeah. I just had no reason to for so long."

He leaned against me and took a step. Though he stumbled, he regained his footing and took another step. "I should have never given up."

"Can't blame you after all that time."

"I didn't even know they were here in the building for the last five years. If I'd had any idea, I'd have been making so much noise. I would have built my strength as much as possible."

"You can't change any of that. Let's just get you out of here. Without magic, this wing is depressing and repressive enough. It's ten times worse with the magic."

Kevin continued leaning against me, and though it felt like it took a week, we finally made our way out into the lit hallway. He covered his eyes immediately. "It's blinding."

"I'm sure it is. Just lean on me, and I'll guide you."

We crept along through the halls. He gained a little more strength the farther we went. Not much, but some. He'd need some food as soon as we made it to the main part of the hotel, which at this rate, could take a week.

I pulled out my phone. Full service again. I called Katya. It went straight to voicemail.

"That's weird. Is she out of range? Did she go back?"

"What?" Kevin asked.

I didn't want to add anything for him to worry about. "Oh, I'm just trying to find Katya. She might've doubled back and missed us."

"We should turn around."

"She'll find us once she sees we're not there. We need to get you food. How are you doing now that you're out of the cursed wing?"

"I can't die in this hotel, remember. Let's go back."

"You need to eat."

"What if Alley and Jennifer are with her?"

"They'll find us." I called Che. It rang, but then went to voice-mail. "Where is everyone?"

"That's what I'd like to know."

I called some of my pack members, but continued only getting voicemails. Irritation ran through me, and I wanted to throw my phone.

Kevin and I were still so far away from the main part of the building. I could order pizza, and by the time we got to the lobby, it'd be cold from waiting so long.

"Do you want me to carry you?"

"No, I need to do this."

"I don't mind."

He ignored my offer. "Are you in love with my daughter?"

I turned to Kevin, surprised by the question. "Come again?"

"Do you love Katya? I picked up that vibe between you two."

"Very much, yes. I've spent the last month trying to keep her safe from your family."

He grumbled at the mention of them. "I appreciate that. And Che's still in the picture? I know it was a lot for me to ask of him to watch them, but as a lone jaguar, he knew why it was important."

"Che hasn't left. He's very protective of them, and they think of him like a father—but they definitely know you're their dad." I cringed at my words. He'd probably feel horrible knowing his kids thought of someone else as their dad, even if it was his best friend.

"It's fine. I wasn't there, so I couldn't expect anything else. I'm just glad it was him rather than anyone else, especially any of my family." He took a deep breath. "But he and Jennifer...? They're not an item?"

"I've never seen anything between them."

Kevin breathed a sigh of relief. "Not that I could blame either of them if they did. I made Che swear he'd watch over the girls if anything ever happened to me. I knew what that could lead to, and I've had nothing but time to think about it."

"Nope. If anything, she's so focused on running the hotel and taking care of the twins, she has no time for anything else as far as I can tell."

"And what about you? How did you come into Katya's life?"

We had nothing but time, so I told him the story of how I'd sensed her years earlier and was immediately worried for a lone female jaguar shifter. Then as her protection spell had weakened, I finally found her, but unfortunately so had their family.

"I'm glad you found her first. You seem like a good kid. What's your story? Where's your family?"

It was my turn to groan. "Not all that different from you, actually. I managed to break free from my family a number of years back."

"And you've been on your own this time?"

"I've joined a pack of mismatched werewolves that also accepts other supernaturals."

"Interesting. And they offer you protection?"

"Like I'm blood. In fact, I need to see if I can get one of them to answer their phone."

"Try Katya again. Or Jenny. I need to talk with her."

"I think we'd probably better find them first."

"Why's that?"

"She and Alley might have to see you to believe you're actually alive."

He grimaced. "That's probably true."

We plodded along in silence for a while. Every once in a while, I tried calling someone. It was futile.

At long last, we reached the hall leading to the main part of the hotel. But at the rate we were traveling, it could be an hour until we reached the rope. Then there was the matter of finding everyone else.

I made more calls. Toby finally picked up.

"Carter, where have you been?"

"Where have *I* been? I've called everyone, only to get voicemails. What's going on?"

"That jaguar shifter pack you've been worried about is in town. Their scent is thick, and people are disappearing."

"What do you mean disappearing?"

"The news—they're reporting about a dozen missing locals."

"You're saying the jaguars are kidnapping humans? Why?"

Kevin looked at me, his expression tight. "Ransom. They want to trade the humans for Katya and me."

"Did you hear that?" I asked Toby.

"Yeah. Is that Che?"

"No, it's actually Katya's dad. Turns out he's not dead, after all."

"And they know it?"

"They're behind it."

"This is worse than I thought. Is Katya with you?"

I took a deep breath. "She was. Clearly, I shouldn't have let her run off on her own. I just thought it'd be quicker for her to find her mom and sister."

"Do you think they got her?"

"Nothing would surprise me at this point. I think we'd better assume they have her."

Toby mumbled something. "Okay, I'll call Gessilyn. We need more than a cloaking spell now. I'll talk to you soon."

"Wait. Have someone bring food."

"How can you think of eating at a time like this?"

"Kevin needs it. He hasn't eaten in twenty years."

Silence.

"Toby?"

"Yeah, I'll have someone send food. He really hasn't had food in two decades?"

"Nope."

He swore. "They have to be working with witches, too. That's the only explanation."

"I'd say that's a good assumption."

We ended the call, and I turned to Kevin. "Since your family is holding people hostage, you think that means they want Katya and you?"

"I know it. They've pulled this before. It's practically their signature move."

My insides tightened. "And what will they do to the innocent people if they don't get you and Katya?"

He held my gaze. "Kill them all—unless we kill those jaguars first."

Chapter Twenty-Six

Katya

A SEARING PAIN RAN FROM BEHIND MY RIGHT EYE TO MY EAR, and then radiated out to the rest of my head. I wanted to rub my temple, but my body was too heavy to move. Even my eyelids were too much effort to open.

I moaned, but the sound didn't make it beyond my throat.

What had happened? Where was I?

Whatever I lay on was hard as a rock. Had I been knocked over and was now resting on the ground? But where?

I sniffed the air. It didn't smell like anywhere familiar. Not the hotel or anywhere on campus I was familiar with. Nor was it Carter's mansion or that supernatural bar in the woods.

The floor felt strange. It vibrated.

Vibrations?

There was a sudden jolt, and I rolled over onto my back and bumped into something.

Was I in a car?

I struggled to open my eyes. It was so dark, I may as well have still had my eyes shut.

Another jolt. I rolled back onto my stomach.

The vibrations stopped. An engine cut. Doors slammed shut. Muffled conversation sounded.

What was going on? Desperation clawed at me as I tried to remember how I'd gotten into the situation.

The volleyball game? No, that'd been a while ago. Finals? Those were done. Then Carter had taken me on that romantic picnic. That had been amazing. One of the best events in my life. A sweet memory I'd always treasure.

Another door slammed, bringing me back to the present. I was locked in a car's trunk and had no idea how I'd gotten there.

Then it hit me.

I'd found my dad. My supposedly-dead dad. He was alive! But my mom and sister had thought I'd lost my mind. The only thing I'd actually lost was my sense of direction inside that maze of halls.

She'd been in contact with my grandpa, who had claimed to have a doctor who could help me with my supposed craziness.

Terror ripped through me. I was trapped in the trunk of a car, and outside were members of my dad's family. Horrible, barbaric people who wanted to force me into a marriage where I'd be nothing more than a slave and baby-making factory.

I had two options. Either I could thrash around and try to bust out or I could lay still and take them by surprise when they opened the trunk. Neither option was ideal. They were just outside, and there were more of them than me.

Unless there was a third option. What if I shifted inside the trunk and attacked them when they came for me? They'd not only be surprised, but in human form.

They wouldn't stand a chance.

I'd be cramped as I waited in jaguar form, but it'd be worth it if I could get away and maybe take a few of them out, too.

I listened, trying to hear what they were saying. If I was going to remove my clothes, I needed to know that I had enough time to shift before they opened the trunk.

No matter how hard I concentrated, everything they said was muffled. I couldn't make out a single word. It was like trying to hear someone speak when under water—something I was all too familiar with after nearly being drowned by invisible hands.

I had some luck.

Not only that, but I probably only had a little time to make my decision. Shift or not? Staying in my human form seemed like a horrible choice. They could too easily overpower me.

I undid my pants and slid them down to my ankles. They wouldn't go any farther. I pushed and kicked, but my ankles wouldn't part.

They'd tied my ankles together.

Someone hit the trunk from the outside.

Did they know what I was doing? I quickly pulled my pants back up and my mind raced. There was no time to disrobe. I just needed to shift.

I closed my eyes and focused on turning.

Nothing happened. Not even a sore muscle. No bones popped.

Maybe I was doing something wrong.

I tried calling to my inner jaguar like Carter said the were-wolves did with their wolf halves.

Nothing.

I focused on my anger. My fear. Stressful emotions usually caused the start of a shift. That was when my bones always started popping before I knew why.

Not this time. Even though I was being held against my will, it wasn't enough to press a shift.

Then I remembered the needle. Whatever had been injected in me probably prevented me from shifting.

So much fury tore through me, I could have exploded. I should have been able to turn into a jaguar ten times over with all my anger.

Yet not even one bone popped.

The sound of a key sliding into a keyhole sounded. I wanted to tear off the face of the next person I saw, but I needed to think clearly.

These people probably expected me to be awake. Angry. To fight back. They'd see that coming a mile away.

Just as the trunk started to open, I closed my eyes and let my body fall limp.

"She's still asleep."

"I told you that was too much solution for her. She's weak. Been raised by humans. Probably never even shifted."

Laughter.

Rage tore through me, but I managed to lay still. I had the advantage of surprise. They didn't expect me to shift and they didn't think I was awake. One way or another, I would use that to my advantage.

Hands slid under my side and back, and someone hefted me up, throwing me over his shoulder. He kept hold of me by keeping his hands pressed against my thighs.

"She's surprisingly muscular." His voice vibrated against me.

"It's gotta be from playing volleyball."

"No, stronger than that. Like she's shifted already."

"That isn't surprising. She's almost twenty, and she's been hanging out with that jaguar who thinks he's a werewolf."

More laughter roared. Gravel crunched underfoot as everyone started walking. The man holding me slid his grasp of my legs higher and higher with each step he took.

He had to be the one who thought he owned me. Who thought I'd be his wife and obey his every wish.

The man had no idea just how wrong he was. As soon as I had the chance, I would take off. With any luck, he'd set me down while we were still outside. Then I could run off, surprising them.

His hold on me kept moving. It took every ounce of my self-control to keep from beating on him. The moment he thought I was awake was the moment I lost surprise being on my side. He could cop a feel now, but that was all he was getting.

He stopped walking. Wood creaked. He stepped up, making my legs bump into someone in front of him. More creaking steps, then a door opened, the hinges squeaking.

I cracked open my left eye to see where we were.

All I saw was another eye of someone right behind the man carrying me.

"She's awake!"

So much for having the element of surprise. I closed my eye and continued playing unconscious. Maybe they'd think the hollering guy was wrong.

"She's awake!" he continued.

"Get her inside."

There was a blur of commotion as numerous hands wrapped around me, pressing me against the guy carrying me.

I was thrown onto a bed. A door slammed shut. Someone pinned my wrists together and pressed me down on the bed, breathing hot tomato breath on my face.

It took all my effort not to turn away. I *had* to convince them I was still unconscious.

"Are you sleeping?"

Slap! A hand across my face.

Somehow I managed not to react, other than my head moving along with the assault.

"Are you awake?" Spittle hit my face.

I refused to respond.

"Rob, you're an idiot!"

"She opened her eye! I saw it. I swear."

"And I swear you're a fool."

Slap! My face throbbed as it was hit on the other side.

"Answer me, woman."

Oh, how I wanted to punch him. He was making it harder and harder for me to fake unconsciousness.

"She's awake! She is," Rob insisted. "Try consummating your marriage early. I bet she'll fight."

My stomach lurched. He wouldn't.

Smack!

That wasn't me. And my ankles were now free.

"Shut up. You just want to watch."

Laughter.

I cracked open my eye. Three men were in the room, and they all had their backs to me.

The door was only a few feet away.

I jumped up and lunged for it.

Chapter Twenty-Seven

Carter

"WANT SOME MORE?" I DUG INTO THE PICNIC BASKET ON THE coffee table between Kevin and me that Laura had brought over. We sat in the lobby while he ate. I pulled out a glass container. "Looks like some stew here."

Kevin nodded, his mouth still full from the half roast-beef sandwich he'd just stuffed in his mouth. He'd already downed a container of macaroni salad and eaten all the meat off a roasted hen.

Apparently nineteen years without food did that to a shifter.

He took a deep breath between bites. "You know, each thing I eat gives me so much more strength. I almost feel as good as I did twenty years ago."

"That's a relief. Keep eating. We have plenty."

Kevin wasn't only gaining strength, but also weight. I could see him filling out with each bite he took. He was nearly as big as me now.

My phone buzzed with a text from Toby.

We picked up Katya's pack scent on the other side of the woods. Hers was mixed in with theirs.

I stared at the text in disbelief.

"Waf?" Kevin swallowed his food. "I mean, what?"

I couldn't find the words. Even though I hadn't been able to get ahold of Katya, I'd assumed she was still in the hotel.

Before I could process that, Jennifer and Alley walked down the stairs. Kevin had his back to them. They walked over and stood behind him, staring at me.

"You should probably go now, Carter," Alley said.

My brows came together. "What do you mean? Am I not welcome here?"

Jennifer stepped forward. "That's not it, but Katya isn't here. She won't be back for some time."

My mind spun, trying to make sense of what had happened. Why didn't Katya's mom seem concerned that she was gone?

Kevin spun around.

Jennifer stared at him, her mouth gaping and her face paling. She stumbled forward. Her mouth moved, but no words came. She fell toward the floor.

Kevin leaped up and caught her. "My Jenny, you look exactly the same."

"Kevin? You... you're alive?"

"Katya was right," Alley whispered.

Kevin swept some hair from Jennifer's face and kissed her. "I've been here in the hotel this whole time."

"But, but... How's that possible?"

He walked her over to the couch where he'd been sitting and held her close. "Baby, there's a lot about my family that you need to know. I don't know where to start..."

Jennifer sat up straight. "Like what? Katya's with your father."

Kevin jumped back. "She's *what?*"

"He said she had a mental illness. That it ran in your family." Tears filled her eyes. "I never should have believed him, should I? It's like something came over me..." She paused. "Wait. He gave me something to drink when we talked. Then suddenly everything he said seemed to make so much sense."

"You can't blame yourself. You were only trying to help our daughter. Now tell me everything. Don't leave out a single detail."

While she told us the whole crazy story, I texted back and forth with Toby to find out how close they were to Katya.

"Is she going to be okay?" Alley asked me.

"I'm going to do everything in my power to make sure she is." I continued texting with Toby.

"So, what's going on if it's not mental illness?"

"You wouldn't believe me if I told you."

"I just found out that my dad's actually alive—and he's been living here this whole time. Whatever you have to say can't be weirder than that."

"I'm going to leave that up to him to tell you. Better yet, Katya."

She huffed. "Who are you texting?"

I hesitated. No matter how I said it, it'd sound weird. I was talking to my alpha. Her sister's math professor.

"What's going on?" Kevin asked.

I glanced up from my phone. "I have a lead. You and Che should come with me, but Jennifer and Alley should stay here."

"Sexist much?" Alley glared at me.

"Trust me, it has nothing to do with that."

She folded her arms. "Right. The men are going to save Katya while the women stay here. What should we do? Make dinner? Knit?"

"It's dangerous. There's a whole world of things you don't understand."

"Whatever. You aren't keeping me from helping my sister."

I glanced at Kevin.

He gave me a slight nod and turned to Alley. "We wouldn't dream of keeping you from helping. You two look around here, and we'll track down my family."

I rose. "And to prove how un-sexist I am, I'll have Alex and Bobby come over here."

Alley arched a brow. "Because Mom and I need protecting?"

I threw my arms into the air. "What do you want? I'm trying to help—and I need to get out there to find Katya!"

"Just let me help!"

I turned to Kevin. "If you want to explain your... family dynamics to them, go ahead. I'm going to find Katya." I didn't wait for a reply. We were wasting too much time as it was, and I wasn't going to let another second slip by while she was in danger.

I raced out the door and sniffed the air. The slightest trace of her scent lingered. It headed toward the woods.

Several of my bones popped.

"Not just yet." I followed the trail until it came to a dead stop a couple blocks away in a small parking lot. They'd taken her somewhere by car.

Great.

I closed my eyes and sniffed the air, holding it in my nose. The trail ended here, right where they'd forced her into a car.

There had to be more to go on. Some other clue. Something. Except that there wasn't anything. No stray items left. Nothing.

I called Toby. "They took her by car. I can't tell what direction they went."

"Killian's here, and he's running a locator spell."

"What about Gessilyn?" Her husband was a well-respected witch, but we needed the high witch at a time like this.

"She's working on something back at home. Some of her other family members are preparing some other spells."

"Tell me the moment you know anything."

"Of course. And Tap's working on something, too. He was speaking too fast for me to understand, so I don't know what. You can try talking to him."

"Not when he's that frantic. I'm going back to the hotel." I ended the call and headed over.

Kevin and Che were both putting on coats. Jennifer and Alley were nowhere in sight.

"Find anything?" Kevin asked.

I shook my head. "I followed her scent to an empty parking lot. They took her somewhere, but where is anyone's guess."

"I know exactly where they took her."

"You do?" I gave him a double-take.

"Our family has a cabin in the woods about fifty miles from here. It's rarely used, but I'm sure that's where she is."

I tugged on my sleeves. "Should we drive or shift?"

He cracked his neck and then twisted his body, sending popping noises down his spine. "I don't know about you two, but I could really use a shift about now."

"Probably faster, anyway." Che unbuttoned his shirt.

"What about clothes to change into?" I asked.

"We're shifters." Kevin slid off his jacket. "We have outfits all around the cabin for miles. They might be out of date, but they'll do the job."

"Sounds good to me. Let's not shift right here, though."

We headed outside.

Chapter Twenty-Eight

Katya

SOMEONE SLAMMED INTO MY BACK, THROWING ME FORWARD. I crashed into a wall, and a framed photo landed on my head. The corner dug into my scalp. Warm blood oozed out.

"Get her!"

I picked up the heavy frame and threw it at the guy about to grab me. It sliced his cheek diagonally. I spun around and ran down the dim hall.

Voices sounded on both sides of the hallway.

I was trapped.

They would be doubly pissed that I'd gotten out of the bedroom.

I darted into the nearest room and closed the door behind me. It was pitch black. I didn't dare turn on the light on the off chance that no one had seen me come inside.

My eyes started to adjust, but not quick enough. I felt around. My fingers found something cool and smooth. It was a dresser. I raced over to the other side and pushed, blocking the door.

It wouldn't keep them out long, but it would buy me a couple minutes at the very least. If that.

I put my hands back out in front of me and walked toward the opposite side of the room. With any luck, there'd be a window.

Smack!

I'd walked right into a bed. It was too low, and I hadn't felt it with my hands.

Voices on the other side of the door called out.

They'd heard me hit the bed.

The door opened, banging into the dresser. It crashed back and forth between it and the door frame.

My throat closed up. A rib popped.

Please wait until I get outside. Please.

I scrambled around the bed and felt around until I came to the wall. There had to be curtains. There just had to be. A shelf. Another one. A desk.

The door continued banging against the dresser. Yelling and swearing.

I felt fabric. Curtains and a window. I scrambled around the curtain, pulling it behind me. My palms pressed against the cool glass. I yanked on the window in the off chance it was unlocked.

It wasn't. I felt around for the lock, unable to see from either the room or the moonlight outside. The woods were too thick on this side of the house.

More banging. Yelling.

Slide.

The dresser moved over the carpeting.

I felt around some more for the lock. It had to be close.

Bang! Bang!

"We're going to get you. Your fiancé is going to make you pay for this insolence!"

Several of my ribs popped. My muscles tightened. If I wasn't so determined to get away from them, I'd spin around and fight them just to prove them wrong. Nobody would ever treat me like that.

My fingers found a curved knob near the middle of the window. That had to be the lock.

Bang, bang!

Slide. Slide.

The dresser fought against the carpeting, but it was a losing battle.

I pressed against the lock. It didn't budge. I tried twisting it. Again, nothing.

Slide...

Beads of sweat formed on my forehead. I tried twisting the lock the other way.

It twisted.

"There she is!"

Rays of light shone in from the other side of the curtain.

My throat dried. I yanked on the window as hard as I could. It slid slightly open.

Bang, slide.

They were still fighting with the dresser—and probably almost had it out of the way.

I pulled against the window. It barely budged each time I pulled with all my strength.

Footsteps thundered toward me.

I yanked on the window. It budged, like it was stuck on something.

Voices yelled over each other. Hands grasped my legs and side.

I gave the window all I had. It opened another inch, but the hands on me thrust me backward. I got caught in the curtain. It twisted around my head. My arms flung out, simultaneously fighting it and the men.

The curtain rod fell to the ground just behind me, allowing the fabric to break free of my face.

Three men had a hold of me. It was three against one in a home they knew well.

I screamed at the top of my lungs.

They pulled me to the ground. I struggled, kicking and hitting. My bones continued popping. Muscles burned.

"She's going to shift!"

"Hey, you've got a fighter. Sure you can handle her?"

Laughter.

I kicked one in the face. The other two tackled me. I resisted with everything in me. They had me outnumbered, but that didn't mean I was going to make it easy on them.

Someone pinned my hands together. They wrapped a rope around my wrists—tightly.

I grimaced and continued kicking. "I'm never going to submit to your backward, archaic rules. Ever!"

"That's what you think." A fist struck my cheek.

"I won't! You may as well give up now. I grew up in the real world, and I refuse to live by your ways." I kicked and kneed at them.

"James likes a challenge."

I yelled out, bit the nearest arm, and continued kicking and kneeing them. Someone pinned me back against the floor and jammed fabric in my mouth. I tried spitting it out, but they taped my mouth shut.

More of my bones popped. It was only a matter of time before I turned and ripped them apart, assuming they didn't also shift.

I kicked and struggled as best I could, but someone pulled me up over his shoulder. My legs were still free, so I kicked as wide and as hard as I could. The position made it that much harder.

They took me to the bedroom I'd been in before. He threw me onto the same bed I had already escaped from.

I was back where I'd started.

"You keep an eye on her, Josh."

One of the men pressed his hands on my arms, pinning me to the bed. "You got it."

The other two left, grumbling and slamming the door behind them.

I fought and struggled, but it did no good considering how tightly I was bound.

"I don't want to be here, either," he said.

What game was he trying to play? I struggled against him all the more.

"Hey, I'm serious. I'm sick of the old ways."

I glared at him. Why was he telling me this? Just to get me to calm down? As if I'd give him that much.

"You don't believe me? I can't blame you, but maybe we can try to get out together. Will you put in a good word for me with your jaguar friends out there if I can get you out?"

Was he for real? I stopped struggling—exactly what he wanted —and studied him.

His expression seemed genuine.

Not that I was going to buy into it for a second. I'd read enough books to know about the whole good cop, bad cop routine. They'd chosen the youngest guy there, thinking he'd be the most convincing. He couldn't even have been old enough to drive.

Too bad they didn't know who they were dealing with—me.

I may have been related to them, but that was exactly where our similarities ended.

"Hey, if you stop struggling, I'll take that tape off your mouth."

Was he serious?

Knock, knock!

"How's it going in there?"

"She's still struggling!"

Laughter. "Well, this is good practice for when you get your own fiancée. You have to teach them being feisty comes with consequences."

More laughter. It faded as they walked away.

The kid leaned closer to me. "I'm serious. This is our chance to get out of here. I want to experience the world. You don't want to be part of ours. Let's work together."

I stared at him. I'd stopped struggling.

Could I trust him? It had to be a ploy.

It just had to be.

He ripped the tape off my mouth. I started to cry out in pain, but he covered my mouth with his palm and shook his head. "Can't let them know I'm doing this."

Then he pulled the fabric from my mouth.

I gagged and gasped for air. "How do I know I can trust you?"

"Have I hurt you? Or helped you?"

"You're with them." I clenched my jaw.

"So was your dad. More and more people have been escaping since he left. Our leaders are furious. He basically started a mini-revolution."

I narrowed my eyes. "For all the good it did him. He's been locked away from everyone for my entire life."

"You know about that?"

I glared at him. "I'm the one who found him."

He studied me. "They said he was protected by an impenetrable spell. How'd you do it?"

"Because I fight until I get what I want."

"And we both want out of here. If we hurry, we can do that."

My pulse pounded. "If this is a trap..."

He shook his head. "It's not. I swear."

I struggled to sit up. "Then prove it. Untie me, then let me tie *your* wrists while I open that window."

"Or." He jutted his jaw. "I take care of the window, then untie you, and we both climb out."

"My idea is better." I narrowed my eyes.

His nostrils flared. "If we don't work together, and soon, we're going to be stuck here. You're going to have to marry a jerk that I guarantee you'll hate. He *will* force you into a life of submission. Your entire existence will be to serve him. Once married, there's no escape."

"So I've been told."

He leaned closer to me. "Then you understand the seriousness of this. You're going to have to trust me or not. Do you want to be the wife of a traditional jaguar shifter, or do you want to live in freedom?"

I glared at him. "This better not be a trick."

"The only thing I want is to get away from these people."

One of my ribs popped. "Untie me."

"You'll put in a good word for me?"

"If you get me out of here safely, then yes."

He untied my wrists.

Chapter Twenty-Nine

Carter

I SNIFFED THE AIR. "HER SCENT IS COMING FROM THE SAME direction we heard the screams."

Kevin sniffed. "She's with a handful of my family members. We have to hurry."

"Is this the direction of that cabin?" Che asked.

Kevin nodded. "It isn't far."

I reached into a pocket for my phone only to realize it wasn't there. I'd had to leave it in my car, close to where we'd left our clothes to shift. Now I wore an itchy outfit we'd found about a mile back. And Kevin had been right—everything was sorely out of style.

Before leaving my phone, I'd told Toby everything I knew, including where the cabin was located. He said he'd pass the information on to Tap and Gessilyn.

The thought of Katya being held captive by the traditional jaguars sent waves of fury through me. What were they doing to her, given they thought they owned her? I shuddered at the thought.

I'd make them pay. Whatever they did to her, I would double onto them. They would regret ever crossing paths with me.

"We're getting close." Kevin's voice broke through my thoughts.

"What's the plan?" I turned to him. "Bust in and take them down?"

"I was thinking more along the lines of figuring out which room she's in and then breaking her out."

"That works, too."

Che froze. "Do you hear that?"

Kevin and I paused.

Footsteps.

The hairs on the back of my neck stood on end. Someone was close, and moving quickly.

"Who's there?" Che called out.

My muscles burned as I prepared to shift at a moment's notice.

Muffled voices sounded.

Kevin, Che, and I exchanged concerned glances. I clenched my fists and prepared for the worst.

Jet, Bobby, and Alex stepped out between some bushes. They all jumped into defensive positions, but then relaxed.

"Did you find them?" Jet asked.

"That way." Kevin nodded in the direction we were heading.

"Where's Toby?" I demanded.

"He's waiting with the witches. Gessilyn is finishing up a spell that should render the jaguars unable to shift for a while."

"Including us?" I exclaimed.

"Not if you stay out of the way."

"What about Tap? Is he coming?"

"As far as I know. He was calling in some favors."

I raked my fingers through my hair. "So, in other words, it's just us for now."

"Pretty much."

"Let's do this."

"What are you wearing?" Bobby arched a brow. "You guys look like you just stepped out of *Dirty Dancing*."

I glared at him. "We had to borrow clothes. Come on. Focus. We have to save Katya."

"*Save* me?"

I whirled around. Katya stood behind me with some kid. I threw my arms around her and spun her in a circle. "I've never been happier to see anyone in my entire life!"

"Me too, but we have to go!"

"They're right behind us," said the kid. "They're going to find us if we don't leave."

Kevin stood taller and tightened his expression. "Good."

"Good?" Katya exclaimed.

"It's time we confront them."

"We're outnumbered!" Katya pleaded with her eyes. "They have weapons."

Kevin turned to the new kid. "You take her to safety. We're going to deal with them."

Katya's mouth dropped open. "Why? I'm away from them. Let's go."

I held her close. "They're never going to give up. We have to face off with them."

The new kid shook his head vigorously. "The rest of the family is headed this way. They want to fight. We don't stand a chance."

I glared at him. "There's no other choice. We have to fight them, or they'll never back down. As in, ever. They'll keep coming after Katya, after Kevin, and now after you. If we don't take them down, they're only going to get worse. You should know that if you grew up with them."

"We can hide."

"That doesn't work," Kevin said. "Nobody knows that more than I do."

Katya pulled away from me and took his hand. "But we can fight them later. On our terms."

"We already have people headed our way. They're going to help us. Soon, we'll outnumber them."

She turned to me. "You can't be in on this, can you? Letting my dad fight?"

"You think I can't hold my own?" Kevin arched a brow.

"I think you need time, Dad. Just hours ago, you were bound to that bed."

"And now I'm not. You're more than welcome to head back. Your mom and sister are worried about us. Not that I can blame them. We can't tell them about us being shifters."

"Cloaking spells," Katya said. "We can carry on with those. They've worked for—"

I shook my head. "That's no way to live."

She turned to me. "I can't ask my dad to jump into this after all he's been through."

"Nobody's asking me," Kevin said. "This is my fight. I'm the one who decided to walk away. I knew the consequences, and I'm still willing to fight for them. Now I actually stand a chance with all you guys on my side."

"That's what you think."

We all spun around toward the voice.

Three groups of about ten shifters each stepped out between the trees.

They outnumbered us.

Chapter Thirty

Carter

CLICK, CLICK, CLICK, CLICK.

They not only outnumbered us, but they had guns. We'd been forced to leave everything behind when we'd shifted.

One of them stepped forward. "Care to give up now, while you still have your lives?"

Kevin moved toward him. "Not a chance. You can't have me or my daughter."

"That's where you're wrong."

The two men stepped even closer to each other, staring one another down.

"Get over here, Josh. Did our captive drag you away?"

Some of the other guys laughed.

"Hardly." The new kid stepped closer. "I'm done with you guys. I want to live out in the world. Away from your backward rules."

"Nobody leaves our family and lives to tell the tale."

"Kevin did." Josh glared at him.

"And that ends tonight. Last chance, kid. Make the right decision."

"I am." Josh stood taller.

"Your funeral." He aimed his gun at Josh's face.

I jumped at the gunman, knocking his weapon out of his grasp. He stumbled but didn't fall. The gun slid away, and Josh lunged for it.

Shots rang out all around.

I leaped toward Katya to protect her.

Bones popped all around as our side turned into jaguars and wolves, then jumped toward our gunned assailants.

I turned to Katya. "Run!"

"Not a chance." She spun around and pulled off her shirt. "I'm fighting in this battle."

Trees rustled just behind me. *Not more of Kevin's family.* I spun around, prepared to attack with my fists.

Toby and some members of our pack pushed through the trees.

Relief washed through me as I raced over to them. "They're not going to give up without bloodshed. Typical traditional shifters."

Toby nodded knowingly. "Gessilyn's coven isn't far behind." He handed me a ten-inch blade. "And we brought weapons."

Howls, growls, and other sounds of fighting grew louder behind me.

I held the knife in position. "We'd better do this."

In a blur, we all raced for the other shifters. A new group of men marched over.

We were outnumbered again. I ran toward the nearest one, aiming the knife for his chest.

He punched me across the face. His ring sliced through my skin all the way from my ear to my nose.

I dug the blade in as far as it would go.

He spat on my face before crumpling to the ground.

Before I had time to wipe the spit from my eye, two more attacked me in a flash of fists.

I swung the knife into one neck while kicking the other guy in the groin. Blood sprayed on me as I yanked the blade out.

He sputtered and crashed to the ground, cursing me. His friend threw himself on me, knocking us both to the ground. We wrestled, and I couldn't dig the knife into any major organ.

"You may as well give up," he grunted.

"Not until you leave Katya alone."

"Over our dead bodies." He shoved my head against a rock.

"If that's what it comes down to." I lunged the blade into his side. Blood immediately darkened his shirt and pooled to the ground. His grip on me weakened.

A pistol lying on the ground in the middle of where the shifted jaguars and wolves fought caught my attention. I jumped up, easily escaping the hold of my dying attacker, and scrambled for the gun.

Jaguars leaped through the air and rolled around on the ground, fighting each other. One nearly knocked me over, but I managed to grab the pistol.

A hand rested on my shoulder. I spun around and aimed the hopefully-loaded gun.

Gessilyn.

I relaxed and dropped my arms. "You made it."

She gave a slight nod and handed me a small vial. "Drink this."

"What is it?"

"It'll make your blood sour—whether you're in this form or if you shift." She glanced around. "Is Katya here?"

I waved toward the mass of fighting animals. "She shifted already."

Gessilyn handed me another vial. "Give this to her. Or do you think you'll shift? In that case, I'll hang onto it."

"I'm not sure yet." I opened and swallowed my potion. It was bitter and bubbled as it went down my throat. "That's awful."

"It isn't nearly as bad as it'll be for anyone who bites you."

I wiped my mouth. "How many came with you?"

"Killian and Frida."

"Can you cast any spells on these guys?"

She glanced around. "It's going to be challenging with everyone fighting together. Anything I cast on them will also fall on our side."

A group of ten barged in through the trees. The one in front cracked his knuckles and glared at us.

"I don't suppose you know them?" Gessilyn asked.

My stomach twisted in knots. "Nope."

"Good."

Good?

She pulled something from her cloak and threw it at them, whispering in a foreign language. A pink mist covered the men and settled on them. They all froze in position.

"That won't last too long, but it'll buy us some time."

One of the jaguars yelped.

I recognized that voice.

Katya.

My heart jumped into my throat. Then anger ran through me. Why hadn't I insisted on taking her away from here? She didn't have experience fighting shifters.

Yelp! Yowl!

I clenched my fists and prepared to shift.

Just as my bones began popping, Tap arrived with some others. The timing couldn't have been better, because another group arrived from the other direction.

Gessilyn spun in their direction and threw a pink mist at them, chanting in a foreign language.

Everything became clearer as I looked around with my jaguar eyes.

Katya cried out again. I bolted in her direction and rammed myself into the jaguar who had his teeth buried into her neck.

He let go but barely stumbled before lunging for her again.

I roared as loud as I could.

He froze and turned toward me, his pupils dilating and hairs standing on end.

I bared my teeth and howled, warning him to flee.

Unfortunately for him, he didn't budge. I leaped on top of him, digging my teeth into his flesh and rolling onto the ground.

We stopped, slamming into a tree. He bit into my back. Pain seared from the wound, but before I could react, he pulled away yelping.

Gessilyn's potion.

I jumped to all fours and growled. *How'd you like that?*

What's in your blood?

Wouldn't you like to know? I jumped on top of him, tearing into his throat. Blood filled my mouth until he went limp. I spit out the liquid and spun around to find Katya.

She rolled around with a different jaguar. But that wasn't what sent a chill through me. Behind the fighting animals, at least fifty humans faced off—most of whom I didn't recognize.

Had Kevin's father brought in his entire family as well as other jaguar families? We were even more outnumbered than before.

Even with the high witch and a former troll king on our side, those were horrible odds. Deadly, even.

For all of us.

Gunshots rang out.

Yelps and cries sounded all around.

The metallic odor of blood hung in the air.

Another jaguar jumped on top of Katya. The three of them rolled around, kicking up dust. Growling and howling ensued.

A low and furious roar escaped my throat. In one quick motion, I ran toward them, slamming into one of them.

He turned on me, digging his teeth into my side. Before I had time to react, he yelped and scurried off. Mid-stride, he crumpled to the ground.

Was my blood growing more potent as the potion lingered?

I thrust myself against Katya's attacker.

He flew into another jaguar, who immediately tore into him.

Katya struggled to her feet.

Are you okay?

Never better. She licked a bloody patch of fur. *You?*

Ready to get you home.

She shook her head. *I'm not leaving until this is finished.*

Have you seen how many people they have?

I don't care. Like you said, we have to make it clear they can't have Dad and me.

To the left, a pink glow covered a group of men.

Katya glanced over then turned back to me. *What's that?*

The high witch is friends with your professor.

And she's here?

I nodded. Something caught my attention.

Just behind her, a jaguar leaped through the air, headed straight for her.

There was no time to warn Katya. I flew over her and crashed into the other jaguar. We fell to the ground. He landed on top of me, and a sharp rock dug into my side.

We rolled around, growling and clawing one another. I just needed him to bite me. He seemed uninterested. Did he know my blood was practically poison?

I turned my head, giving him an easy shot to my neck.

He bit down, but didn't yelp or cry out.

Chapter Thirty-One

Katya

TERROR RAN THROUGH ME AS CARTER OFFERED HIS NECK TO the other jaguar. My instincts kicked in as soon as the jerk bit down.

I roared—a sound so terrifying it sent a shiver down my own spine. Then I lunged through the air and slammed into the jaguar. He sputtered, spraying blood all over my face.

We rolled onto the ground and crashed into a tree. The image of him digging into Carter's flesh was seared into my mind. I dug my teeth into the creature, eager to kill him.

Once he went limp, I spat out the blood and looked around for Carter. What I saw in the distance sent a chill of fear through to my core.

Even more men arrived from the direction of the cabin. They marched toward us like they were on a mission. And they were—a mission to kill me and the ones I loved.

There had to be ten times more of them than us.

Everything spun around me and I struggled to breathe. Had we underestimated them? Even if we had witches and whoever Tap had brought, did we stand a chance?

Or would it be better if I gave myself up in order to save everyone else?

As much as I hated the thought of joining my dad's family as someone's property, maybe it was for the best. They might even let my dad go back to Mom and Alley if I handed myself over.

I stood taller and glanced around, trying to tell if I could see who was in charge.

A spine-chilling roar rang through the air.

Something primal inside of me told me that was the roar of an alpha. He was the one I needed to turn myself in to so I could save everyone else.

He roared again, and I spotted him near the humans.

I turned to Carter. *I love you.*

Wait. What are you doing?

The realization that I'd never see him again nearly crushed me. I spun away from him and bounded toward the alpha, stopping just a foot away. Then I knelt and pressed my nose to the ground.

Loud flapping sounded in the air above.

Flapping?

I glanced up. Dragons of every shape, size, and color filled the sky, blocking the view of all the trees. Several blew fire, lighting up the entire area.

Carter had said something about Toby having a connection to a dragon king.

In a blur of activity, everyone jumped into action at once. Dragons attacked shifters and people alike. Some even turned into human themselves.

I turned and threw myself at the alpha I'd started to submit to.

He threw me to the ground and pinned me, proving to be far stronger than any of the other jaguars I'd fought.

I struggled to break free, but he wouldn't budge. Carter lunged at him, but bounced right off, skidding on the ground.

The air glowed pink and then orange. Spine-tingling roars

sounded from every direction—warning calls from jaguars, dragons, and wolves. A couple even sounded like bears.

A chill ran through me.

Something hard struck my head. White dots danced before my
eyes. My eyelids closed, blanketing me in darkness.

Chapter Thirty-Two

Katya

A SWEET SMELL TICKLED MY NOSE. I ROLLED OVER. SOFT, WARM blankets enveloped me. So did a pounding in my head. A fluffy pillow seemed to help the aching.

What was that aroma? It made my stomach rumble. Had Che made me breakfast?

Images from the forest flooded my mind. Jaguars, wolves, dragons, bears, witches, and trolls fighting.

I'd bowed before the alpha jaguar to offer myself in exchange for everyone else.

What had happened after that?

Had he accepted the deal? Was I now part of the family as a wife and baby-maker for a tyrannical husband?

My stomach twisted in such tight knots that not even the delicious smell could relax me. Food didn't matter if I now had only a lifetime of servitude to look forward to. It would be worth it if my loved ones were safe—if my mom and dad could finally be together again. At least they would have Alley.

The anticipation was too much. I needed to open my eyes and see where I was. It was time to face reality.

I cracked open one eye. The strange room was dim, but there was enough light to see. I appeared to be alone. At least from the section of the room I could see.

The furniture appeared to be expensive, and everything was tidy.

I opened my other eye and sat up, scanning the room. More pricey items decorated the huge bedroom.

At least if I was going to be forced into a miserable marriage, I'd have nice things.

Somehow, that seemed like little consolation. I was only trying to make the horrible situation seem tolerable. It never would be. Not when my heart would always belong to Carter.

"You're awake."

I froze. The male voice came from right next to me—in the bed.

Fear tore through me.

Why couldn't I have died in the woods?

"Katya." The voice was gentle. Familiar.

I turned toward him. My gaze met the eyes of the man I loved more than life itself under the covers with me. I crumbled back onto the pillow, unable to hold myself up.

Carter brushed hair away from my face. "Are you okay?"

I gasped for air, unable to breathe. The only thing I could do was take in his sight. He was just as gorgeous as ever and had on no shirt. A blood-stained bandage wrapped around his torso.

Finally, I found my voice. "What happened? How'd we get here? Where is here?"

He scooted closer and pressed his lips on mine. "Toby's mansion. We won. The few remaining members of your relatives ran away with their tails between their legs. They aren't coming back."

"Who's left?"

"Not many. I killed their alpha. Not that he made it easy."
Carter rubbed his bandage. "But once the dragons arrived, victory
came quickly. Between them and the witches, the other side didn't
stand a chance."

"What about Josh? He helped me. I hope he's safe."

"He's downstairs—he was a lot of help during the battle, too."

Relief washed through me. I leaned my forehead against his.
"I'm glad you're okay."

He kissed my cheek. "I'm better than okay. You're alive and
well, and those jaguars are gone for good. What more could I
ask for?"

"What about my dad and Che? Your pack?"

"Your dad and Che are back at the hotel. They concocted a
story about a hunting accident. Your mom and sister think you're
helping me recover from that."

Sadness ran through me. "They can never know about us being
shifters?"

Carter shook his head. "Not unless they witness something
that we can't explain away—such as one of you shifting. It's better
that way."

I nodded, understanding but hating it. "What about your pack?
Is everyone okay?"

He cleared his throat. "We weren't without casualties."

I gasped. "You lost family because of this? Who?"

Carter rubbed his thumb along my jawline. "Don't feel guilty.
We all knew what we were getting into."

Tears stung my eyes. "Who died?"

He wiped his eyes. "A couple guys you never met."

"I need to know their names."

Carter cleared his throat again. "Mateo and Dash." His voice
cracked. "They were wolfborns."

It felt like a punch in the gut. "And now they're dead because
of me."

"No, to keep you safe. To stand up for the freedom of shifters everywhere. Anywhere a shifter is in danger, it's a cause our pack stands up against."

I snuggled closer to him, pressing my ear against his bare chest and listening to his heartbeat. No matter how he tried to justify it, good shifters had died for me.

He ran his palm over the length of my hair a few times. "Don't blame yourself. They wouldn't want you to."

"How do you know?"

"Because they were excited to fight for a cause. To help take down people like your fam—your relatives."

I looked at him. "But still. They shouldn't have had to pay the ultimate price."

Carter pressed his mouth on mine and kissed me deeply. It took my breath away, and almost made me forget why I was upset. Almost.

His phone rang, and he reached over to a nightstand. "It's your dad." He swiped his finger across the screen. "Hey, Kevin... Uh-huh... Yeah, sure. Give us an hour."

I arched a brow.

"Okay. See you then." Carter ended the call and set his phone down. "We're going to meet your family at the hotel. Your mom and sister are worried about you."

"I'm sure they are."

He kissed my forehead. "I'll let you get the first shower. That dried blood in your hair will freak them out."

My hand immediately went to the sorest spot on my head. Sure enough, my hair was stiff and a little sticky. "What happened?"

"Someone hit you in the head with a rock while the alpha had you pinned. I killed him before the alpha."

My heart raced as I stared into the eyes of someone who loved me enough to actually kill for me.

He brushed his lips across mine. "Hurry up and get that shower. I told them we'd be there in an hour."

I held his gaze as I climbed out of bed and headed into the bathroom. Inside, a pile of folded clothes awaited me.

Once dressed, I went back into the bedroom. Carter sat on the perfectly made bed, already showered, a tray of steaming food next to him.

"What's this?"

He smiled. "Laura brought us up breakfast. I'd already put on fresh blankets, so now it's breakfast *on* bed instead of in."

"Sounds good to me." I climbed over and snuggled against him.

Carter picked up a strawberry and fed it to me. I picked one up and dipped it in a little tray of melted chocolate. Smiling, I held it out for him but then took a bite myself.

He laughed. "You're beyond adorable."

"You think that's adorable?"

"I do."

"How about this?" I dipped another strawberry in the chocolate and leaned toward him, but at the last second, I smeared it across his face.

Carter grinned slyly. "Now you have to lick it off me."

"You wish." I put the fruit in his mouth and reached for another.

He dropped it on the tray, wrapped his arms around me and rolled me over. "Yes, I do wish."

My cheeks heated, but I leaned closer and kissed the chocolate from his face. He then covered my face in kisses, stopping at my mouth.

Carter held my gaze. "I love you."

"I love you more."

He pressed his mouth on mine and deepened the kiss right away.

It sent a wave of warmth and excitement through me. My heart raced and threatened to explode out of my chest.

Carter sat up, pulling me with him, and he ran his fingertips from my ear to my chin.

A chill shivered its way across my whole body.

He traced my lips. "I can't live without you. Now that I've

tasted what life is like with you, I'll never be able to go back to my boring, monotonous life."

I kissed his fingertip. "You don't have to."

Carter stared into my eyes with an intensity I could feel to my core. "Will you marry me?"

My mouth gaped and my pulse raced through my body. He wanted to marry me?

"It doesn't have to be today, or even before you graduate. But will you make me the happiest man alive?"

I threw my arms around him and kissed him. "Yes, yes! A thousand times, yes."

He squeezed me tightly, then turned to the tray of food. "Where did Laura put that ring?"

It hadn't been an impromptu proposal? He'd put enough thought into it to get a ring?

Carter dug around behind a napkin. "Found it." He held up a gorgeous sparkling diamond engagement ring and slid it on my finger. "I hope you like it."

I couldn't take my eyes off it. "I love it almost as much as I love you."

"It was my mother's."

I turned to him. "You want me to have your mom's ring?"

He nodded. "As long as you'll have me."

"Forever and for always." I gazed into his eyes. "Where are we going to spend the rest of our lives?"

Carter kissed my nose. "Here. The hotel. I don't care as long as we're together. Maybe we could travel to Central or South America to where the jaguar shifters originated. I've always been curious to visit the old ruins."

"I like the way you think."

His eyes lit up. "We could also check out Egypt. We have a lot of jaguar history there too. In fact, my friend the valkyrie loves it over there. She could show us around—you two will hit it off for sure."

"That sounds like quite the adventure. I'd love to explore the world with you."

I wrapped my arms around him again and kissed him passionately. I couldn't wait to be the wife of the most wonderful jaguar shifter in the world.

Cover Reveal

Renegade Valkyrie Coming May 8, 2018!

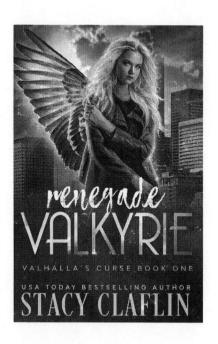

Other Books by Stacy Claflin

If you enjoy reading outside this genre, you may enjoy some of Stacy Claflin's other books, also. She's a *USA Today* bestselling author who writes about complex characters overcoming incredible odds. Whether it's her Gone saga of psychological thrillers, her various paranormal romance tales, or her romances, Stacy's three-dimensional characters shine through bringing an experience readers don't soon forget.

If you like the Curse of the Moon series, you might enjoy the Transformed series where it all began...

Main Books

Deception

Betrayal

Forgotten

Ascension

Duplicity

Sacrifice

Destroyed

Transcend

Entangled

Dauntless

Obscured

Partition

Standalones

Fallen

Silent Bite

Hidden Intentions

Saved by a Vampire

Sweet Desire

The Gone Saga

The Gone Trilogy: Gone, Held, Over

Dean's List

No Return

Alex Mercer Thrillers

Girl in Trouble

Turn Back Time

Little Lies

Against All Odds

Curse of the Moon

Lost Wolf

Chosen Wolf

Hunted Wolf

Broken Wolf

Cursed Wolf

Secret Jaguar

Valhalla's Curse

Renegade Valkyrie

Pursued Valkyrie

Short Story Collection

Tiny Bites

The Hunters

Seaside Surprises

Seaside Heartbeats

Seaside Dances

Seaside Kisses

Seaside Christmas

Bayside Wishes

Bayside Evenings

Bayside Promises

Bayside Destinies

Bayside Dreams

Standalones

Haunted

Love's First Kiss

Fall into Romance

Author's Note

Thanks so much for reading *Secret Jaguar*. I've been looking forward to writing Carter's story since he was first introduced in *Lost Wolf*. It was hard to wait, but it was well worth it! This won't be the last we see of him or the others from the series, however. As was teased in the last chapter, we're likely to see him Soleil's series. (What do you think of that cover? Do you love it as much as I do?)

I can't wait to dig in and start writing Soleil's series. (If you haven't yet read the earlier books in this series, be sure you do. They'll give the background for what has Soleil in so much danger.)

While waiting for the new series, feel free to check out my other books—I've written over 40 at this point. I write in three genres: romance, thrillers, and of course paranormal! Similar themes run throughout most of my books, and many of my readers have found they enjoy new genres because my books tend to have similar undertones no matter the focus.

At this time, I'm writing *When Tomorrow Starts Without Me*, a standalone novel that's slightly different than anything else I've written. It's about a girl name Kenna who has nothing to live for, and when you find out her history, you'll understand why she feels this way. Then she meets Rogan, who shows her life is worth living

—after saving her life. But when Kenna's past won't stop haunting her, will she be able to find the strength to go on? Or will the demons win?

I'd love to hear from you. The easiest way to do that is to join my mailing list (link below) and reply to any of the emails.

Anyway, if you enjoyed this book, please consider leaving a review wherever you purchased it. Reviews will help other readers find my work. They can be short—just share your honest thoughts. That's it.

I've spent many hours writing, re-writing, and editing this work. I even put together a team who helped with the editing process. As it is impossible to find every single error, if you find any, please contact me through my website and let me know. Then I can fix them for future editions.

Thank you for your support! I really appreciate it—and you guys!

Made in the USA
Middletown, DE
09 June 2018